Doug Thompson

CHECKMATE

Portraits of Power

Matador
9 Priory Business Park
Kibworth Beauchamp
Leicestershire LE8 0RX, UK
Tel: (+44) 116 279 2299
Fax: (+44) 116 279 2277
Email: books@troubador.co.uk
Web: www.troubador.co.uk/matador

ISBN 978 1780884 233

British Library Cataloguing in Publication Data.
A catalogue record for this book is available from the British Library.

Printed and bound in the UK by TJ International, Padstow, Cornwall
Typeset in 12pt Aldine401 BT Roman by Troubador Publishing Ltd, Leicester, UK

Matador is an imprint of Troubador Publishing Ltd

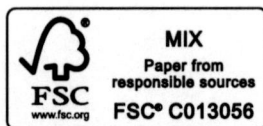

MIX
Paper from
responsible sources
FSC
www.fsc.org
FSC® C013056

For John Gatt-Rutter

and

Gareth Whittaker

in appreciation

£5

CONTENTS

v

"... and behold the tears of such as were oppressed, and they had no comforter; and on the side of their oppressors there was power; but they had no comforter."

Ecclesiastes 4:1

MIND OF GOD

The door opens and, after a little hesitation on the threshold, the man allows himself to be ushered into the shadowy, cavernous, chaotic room.

The young woman follows him in, a few paces behind, and tells him to sit down.

It isn't obvious where she means, so he looks at her, gesturing helplessly, at the same time trying to make sense of the room. She points to a camp stool that is half hidden under a round, formica-topped table. He nods, smiles wanly, and sits. His head is barely visible above the top of the table.

What sort of 'vanity' does *this* 'coming-in' represent? I think, and I have to laugh. *Vermis est eius et non homo.* Well, that's obvious! So why not say it?

He keeps on looking round. Peering round. Squinting round. Trying to make out, piece together. Uneasy from the start. Lost from the start. This interview's going to be… a bit run-of-the-mill…

But… let's watch a while.

The secretary hands him the form to fill in, and a pen. "Was it you who phoned?" she asks.

The man looks up. "Phoned?" he repeats, blinking. "Me?" Then, with a huge effort, transferring his thoughts from the papers where they've already begun to settle, like dust, "No. It wasn't me. My sister phoned for me. It was my sister…"

He puts down the pen, laying it precisely, diagonally across the page. "You see, she saw it advertised… the *Evening Standard*. She thought it sounded just right from the description it gave. I said it sounded all right… just right. So she phoned from the box across the street. Right away. And…"

The secretary turns away. She goes back towards the door. "Just fill in the form while you're waiting", she commands, over her shoulder, before closing the door behind her.

So, we're alone together. But I'm in no hurry. Watching and waiting.

He picks up the papers and holds them close to his eyes. He slews round and brings them closer to the feeble light coming from the naked bulb over the door. I can see him mouthing the words. He's in difficulties already. Then he starts looking round again. Peering round. He makes another, half-hearted effort to get some sense out of the papers, but he's caught between curiosity and an obvious inability to concentrate – with all my experience, I recognise the type easily enough. He puts the form back on the table, absent-mindedly, near the edge, and stands up. He yawns noisily, and stretches, still squinting in the half light.

Then the big light comes on at the far end of the room and the bell rings. One of the players, a milkman, gets up and leaves the room by the right-hand door, and immediately his place is taken by another, a market trader, coming in through the left-hand door, and the game resumes.

The man is obviously startled. By the suddenness of the light, of course. Then by the gradual awareness that they have been there all along and he hadn't noticed. He's trembling ever so slightly. He even backs away a little, but stops when he bumps into the table; he has to grab hold of it to stop it falling over. I have to smile.

I think of starting now but put away the thought at once because he begins, in that moment, to move cautiously over towards the players. The light has, of course, dimmed again, so even a few paces away from them, he still hasn't become aware of the partition that separates them from him. Only when he's right up against it does he realise it's there. In the nick of time. Some of them walk right into it. I think he's going to, but he doesn't. Pity! That bit always makes me laugh. He steps back a couple of paces and stumbles over a pile of boxes and then falls into them... instead. What a noise! What a spectacle! Better than if he'd walked into the glass partition. So, I get my laugh after all. And he gets his reminder… There's a lot of potential here. "Time and chance. Time and chance", I always say.

So, when he's managed to scramble to his feet – wincing, and clutching his left knee – he looks back at the players the other side of the glass, and goes and taps at it. Quietly at first. But when no one notices him, he taps more loudly. And when still no one takes any notice of him, yet more loudly, more insistently, but it profits him not.

They just go on…

He hobbles up and down the length of the partition, trying to find a way in, waving, gesticulating, but no one takes the slightest notice of him, of course. Finally, he goes and stands with his nose pushed up against the glass, watching, captivated – until his own breath so obscures the image that he turns away, with a shrug. How right he is. He makes his way back to the table, but keeps on looking back, obviously bewildered.

Then the light beyond the partition goes out, the bell rings, and by the time the light has come back, a fireman has left and his place has been taken by a butcher – though I doubt if the man notices this fine detail.

He keeps on shaking his head. That's the way it takes most of them.

Only when he's sure that things are back to 'normal' beyond the glass partition does he sit down again and look at the form. He writes a couple of things then he's in difficulty all over again. I can see the pain of ignorance spreading across his face. Impatience at his own ignorance. He throws the pen down and it bounces off the table onto the floor. He swears and tries to see where it has gone. Then, not seeing it because of the light, he goes down on his hands and knees, feeling about for it under the table. He doesn't know about the perversity of things, even now – another of my little jokes they have to contend with. Always. He manages to find it after a minute or so, jerks back up and bangs his head against the under side of the table. He swears some more and rubs his head. What a bang! What a laugh!

He's getting angry, swearing under his breath, slamming about. He even kicks out at a big, multi-coloured medicine-ball, half as big as himself, then he limps off in pain, swearing loudly, even more vehemently, towards the back of the room, but checking every few steps that all is as it should be, as he thinks it should be, the other side of the partition. They're always interested in what's going on, on the other side.

And so it is, at last, he comes face to face with himself in the huge, old-fashioned, floor-to-ceiling mirror, just to the right of the door. The light – such as it is – is all above and to his left, so the shadows start early into the mirror and he squints and he peers, rubbing his breath off its brown-speckled glass with his sleeve.

Through a glass darkly, darkly, ever so darkly.

And then he sees me. A shadow in shadow. But he can't be sure. So he stares hard, into the mirror. Then he steps back a few paces and stares some more.

"Good God!" he gasps, then again, "Good… God!"

"Quite so," I say, "Who else?" And then, in a flash, I think: 'Let there be light', and I snap on the lamp over the tray that serves as a desk on these occasions. Sitting up here, in my high chair, always impresses them. It shocks them and impresses them. And that's how it is with this one. He turns his back on the mirror and stares hard in my direction… it's the effect of the light. Shielded from above it leaves my face in shadow and they're always peering hard to see what I'm really like. It must be quite… unnerving, at times. Keeps them in their place though.

Anyhow, he turns and stares and when he can manage to speak he says, "Have you been there all along… all the time I've been in here?"

"Longer than that even", I say, but he doesn't ask what I mean. They're mostly like that. Can't see beyond the end of their noses. There's no point in delaying things any longer, so I start the… process.

"Name?" I say – the obvious first question in any interview, but it's surprising how it can throw some of them into a miasma of confusion. And he is no exception.

"Name?" he repeats dully. And then: "Ah, well, you see, sir," he says, "I've already put that in this 'ere form. And my address too."

It's not important to me what they call him, just a formality really, whimsy really, so I press on. "Well, that's something," I say, "…so you've already completed the form (knowing full well he has done no such thing). The form is the key."

He edges forward a little, waving the form in his left hand. "Well… no, not exactly, sir. Some things I've put but there were other things I didn't know what to answer… some things, as well, I didn't… rightly understand."

At that I sigh audibly – it never fails to make them feel uneasy, foolish and uneasy, and it does the trick on this occasion.

"I'm sorry, sir," he says, "I got sort of… distracted by… by…" and it's clear he can't remember what he 'got distracted' by. And I think of the talents… Anyhow, just to remind him, I ring the bell, the lights go off the other side of the partition and spaces are vacated and filled in the time-honoured manner. Time and the bell… "…distracted by… all of that through there", he concludes. Then, with a titanic effort of reflection (I am very patient, withholding my rapidly inflating sighs until I almost burst), he asks: "What are they doing – those people through there?"

I shift my position slightly, and squint theatrically to give the impression I'm looking in the direction he is pointing, and after a significant pause I say: "They're playing cards, aren't they?"

"Yes. Yes. They are…" he says, hesitantly, "but why does the light go out and one of them leaves and another comes in?"

"Oh, that", I say, as if it doesn't have all that much importance. "It's just that they're waiting…"

"Waiting for what?" he asks, looking ever more stupid and perplexed.

"To go on", I tell him, and wait then for his reaction.

"On? On what?" his brow puckering under the strain.

"Not 'what' but 'where'?" I say. "They go on when it's their turn. Then come off when they've had it."

At last he thinks he understands and brightens a little. "You mean there's a show going on right now?"

"Oh yes," I say, "right now. Any time at all, in fact. We never close…"

He nods, a bit dubiously, I suspect, but he has neither the wit nor the courage to probe any further. So many of them are like that. I can get away with murder. Truly, I can…

"Right!" I say, forcefully. "Would you let me see the form you've filled in?"

At this he blanches, embarrassed no doubt, and begins to explain over again about how… I cut him short. I'm not going to listen to that rigmarole all over again. Boring is boring, especially if you happen to have aeons of time at your disposal.

"Give it me, nevertheless," I snap, "and I'll help you complete it."

At this he looks grateful, though why he should I can't think, since it's going to expose even further what a miserable little shadow he is.

Looking down the list of questions he hasn't answered, we begin at 'Last Occupation'. I know we are in for another lot of excuses for his inadequacy, even before I ask it. "Ah, yes. Well…" he begins, characteristically. I sigh loudly at his predictability. "I was a barber", he says – with a touch of pride in his voice, if I'm not mistaken. Can I be mistaken?

"A barber!" I exclaim, with more than a hint of incredulity in *my* voice. "Well, that hardly suggests continuity or dedication to a chosen career path, does it?" He shakes his head and looks quite downcast, as though I've caught him out in a lie. "Tell me" – I press hard on his confusion – "how do you see that helping you if your application is successful?"

He shrugs – irritably, it seems. "Don't know," he says, petulantly, "…'cos I don't really know what the job *'ere* is."

I cannot believe what I'm hearing. He really is trawling the depths of fecklessness. This is just too good to pass over.

"You mean to say… " I begin – then repeat it (for effect) – "you mean to say… you've applied for a position without knowing what it is?"

His reply, for once, is wholly unexpected and I'm a bit taken aback by it.

"Not exactly," he says, "since (and on reflection it was this 'since' that got up my nose) I haven't yet put in an application", and he nods towards the incomplete application form on the tray in front of me. "No, I've come *about* the job… to find out what it is… to see whether I'd be right for it. It was my sister, you see. She saw it in the evening paper and thought it sounded like it might be the sort of thing… I'd be good at." He smiles, disarmingly, but I'm in no mood for suffering fools. It crosses my mind to question the logic of his last statement, its incompatibility with his confessed total lack of knowledge about the nature of the… position, but I'd be wasting my time… and anyway, he'll know soon enough… now.

It's in moments like this that I'm forced to contemplate the less than perfect nature of my own handiwork, whatever the wise old theologians say about it. Or maybe it's the price you pay for giving them 'free will' as those same wise old theologians always claimed I did – in this particular case, free will to be utterly unaware that he even possesses it, if he does… The ingratitude! Makes you want to rub them out, right away – and I sometimes do, of course. Anyway, enough of that. So, I pass on to the next part of the question, the 'Reasons for leaving' part, and settle back to listen to yet more of his meanderings.

"We got taken over. That's why I left. You see, there were four of us worked there but the new firm, a chain, said they could only keep three of us on. I didn't think much about it when they said that because I'd been there a lot longer than the others so I knew I was all right. But I'd got it wrong, somehow. The new manager, a nice young fellow – Mr Cameron was his name – came early on Monday morning and told us all how grateful his firm was for our past services, our devotion to our work, our loyalty to the firm… and he hoped that after the transformation, when things had settled down again, that same sense of dedication would continue. The other three all nodded as enthusiastically as they could, but I just sat there nodding ordinary like.

Maybe it was that what did it – not nodding harder, I mean… I don't know. When a customer came in Mr Cameron pointed him to a chair and told young Harry (who had been with us for less than three months, and was still learning) to attend to him. Harry beamed. At least it wasn't him, then.

That was when Mr Cameron asked me to go with him into the rest room at the back.

He didn't beat about the bush none, he come straight out with it. 'Regretfully,' he said, and he really stressed that. '*Regretfully*, Jack, we're going to have to let you go…'

I was stunned, I can tell you. 'Let me go?' I repeated, at a loss to know just what he meant by that… in that moment.

'The reason being that the shop has been losing money for quite some time now and we are going to have to… institute (I think that was the word he used) a new productivity deal – longer hours, less pay per hour, more throughput each day – you know the sort of thing, and… quite frankly, the Board felt it couldn't insult such a long-standing and devoted servant of the old company, such as you have been, by asking you to accept these new conditions. We will, of course, provide you with the highest references – it will be our pleasure.'

"I thanked him for his kindness; he shook my hand warmly; I picked up my coat and cap and went out in a daze. And that was that." And he shrugs at the memory of it.

Then a question that really does take him by surprise: "Do you happen to have brought the reference with you?"

"Reference?" he repeats, clearly perplexed. "Reference?" And at that I remind him about the 'highest reference' he had been promised by his erstwhile employers.

"Oh, that…" he says, then sort of smiles and shakes his head. "I was that upset, you see. Once I realised what had happened. And I didn't go back for it right away. I couldn't face in right away. My pride, you see… Those other younger chaps. Much less experience… Anyhow, by the time I did go back the shop had closed down. It was all boarded up with a 'To Let' notice on it. But I've got over it now… I suppose I must have, by this time."

"And how long ago was that?" I think to ask, with an eye still on the form which will decide things for him, one way or another.

"Oh, that would be… maybe eight years back", he says, nodding his head in agreement with the surmise that has dropped out of it.

"And… since then?" I come back at him, not wishing to lose the advantage to some vague sense he might entertain of sympathy on my part. But he looks blank, repeating the question half aloud, a habit I'm beginning to find very irritating indeed.

Once it's clear he doesn't understand, I repeat it more explicitly. "What have you been doing since you lost your job… as a barber… eight years ago?"

He looks uncomfortable, shifting from one foot to the other, fidgeting with his hands. These signs of inadequacy always make me seethe, make me want to grind them into dust.

After a longish silence he speaks, taking a couple of unadvised steps towards my chair. "A bit of this and a bit of that… sir," he says, without much conviction, "but mainly things around the 'ouse – for the wife. Bits of decorating, changing light bulbs… that sort of thing."

There is another pause, then he adds, "At first I was that mad I went to the Labour Exchange every day – the 'Job Centre', as they call it now, except there aren't any jobs, leastways, there weren't for me. I always had difficulty with the forms, you see. I never did have much time for forms. Didn't have the education, you see; didn't get the schooling, what with my dad being poorly all the time, until he died, then my mother being out at work all hours God sends ('Why blame me?' I'm thinking – a remark that's hardly calculated to endear him to me), I 'ad to stay at home and look after him…

After he'd... gone... I'd missed so much I was terrified to go to school; everybody made fun of me – couldn't read, couldn't write or add up nor nothing of that sort – and especially the teachers, they thought I were a great joke. I hated school. I played truant every chance I got. It did me no good though. I regret it now. I have all my life. Too late now, though. Much too late."

I nod reflectively, wholly in agreement. 'How right you are', I think.

"I once nearly got an interview though," he says then, smiling at the memory of his almost triumph, "only they'd got us mixed up, you see. There were two of us with the same name had applied and they got us mixed up. Anyhow, this chap comes round the day before the interview and explains. He was ever so good about it, apologising all the time. Brought us a couple of tins of baked beans and a bottle of ketchup – the job had been in a firm that made them. It took the edge off the disappointment – at least, until we'd ate all the beans."

'A little lower than the angels', wanders into my mind then 'on wings of eagles' follows it, but I can't remember any of their sayings about beans – if they ever had any! Perhaps as well he has come to judgement.

"I've watched a lot of telly these last few years. Fallen asleep in front of it more times than I can remember. It fills the time. Gets you through to tomorrow. I've read a lot as well, only mostly in secret. The wife doesn't like that. Says it's a waste of time. When I could be doing things in the house or the garden. So generally, I wait till she's out. Or I take a book or a magazine with me when I go to... to... the lav, if you'll pardon the expression, sir. If I speak the truth, sir, I think I was hoping... this job here – whatever it is – would give me some time, some peace, on my own. I'd like that. It's really what I've always wanted in a job. Being on your own. I never was one for talking much at work – though it was part of the job as a barber – but it was always the same conversations (if you can call them that) and you got so you could have them without thinking what you were saying. It wasn't as though the customers wanted to talk much either. It was just sort of expected that you would…"

I think it's about time he's reminded of how things are really, so I ring the bell the other side of the partition and there's a pause in his prattle while he turns and watches the whole sequence through once more, shaking his head from side to side, occasionally glancing back at me as if seeking an explanation – an explanation that is never forthcoming, of course. Never. When it is finished and 'normality' (they love that word – they believe it really does mean something) resumes, I engage him once more… on my terms.

"Now," I say, "you mentioned something about how this situation might suit you. How you've always wanted one like this. Peace. Time to yourself… by yourself… Is that it? Have I got it right?"

He nods vigorously.

"So how would you see yourself fitting in here… not being a team-player?" I ask.

He smiles at this. His eyes seem to glaze over. There's a longish pause while he collects together his few scraps of thought, then he starts. "I'd do my rounds as soon as I got in. Even before I'd got my coat off... Me and the dog. It would be nice to have a dog for company. I've always wanted one but the missus was dead against it. So, anyhow... we'd go round and check everything was all right. Then I'd come back to the hut – if it was a hut – sometimes, nowadays, it's an office inside, with a telephone... And I'd put the kettle on and the dog – Pip, that would be his name... he'd be a collie – would settle down in front of the fire or the stove and maybe have a nap for a bit. I'd get my tea – I drink a lot of tea – in a pint mug, not much milk, three sugars, and I'd sit down and maybe get a book out, or most likely a magazine, till it was time to do the rounds again. Working nights would suit me fine. I wouldn't mind that at all. Going home in the morning I could go to bed and stay there for most of the day. The wife couldn't say nothing about that if I was working nights." Then he stops talking and, after musing for a while, he looks up into my light, blinking, and smiles (foolishly – as is befitting!), "but I don't suppose it's anything at all like that, is it, sir?"

Naturally, I ignore the question, as I always have done. "Right, Mr, Mr, er…" I begin (so he'll get things quickly back in perspective). He mutters something – his name, presumably – but I press on since this is of no consequence to me. "Let us proceed to the interview."

At this, he fingers the knot of his tie, drawing himself up to his full height, standing almost to attention. He glances round too, looking for somewhere to sit, I suppose – curious how they instinctively want present experience to mirror that of their past, or if not always their past, certainly some idea they keep locked away in their miserable little minds of how particular situations ought to evolve…

I think of ringing the bell again, just to add to his confusion, but decide against it for the moment. "Right!" I say again, with a particular… reflective emphasis, "we'll begin with the somersault."

At this he looks startled, as, of course, I intend him to be, not quite sure he has heard correctly, but at the same time not wanting to convey the impression that he has been inattentive – that's how they are, most of them. I let him wrestle with the problem for a moment or two, then press on. "Perhaps it would make for greater efficiency in performance if you were to remove your jacket."

He nods, but I can see he's hesitant, not sure whether he should say something. Having taken off the jacket he looks around for somewhere to put it and decides the best place is the little table near the door, so off he trots, with a silly little half-sidling, half-skipping movement, and is back in a trice, trying to look as though he has never been away. The things that must go through their minds! What was wrong with the floor? After all, that's where he's going and it isn't as though the jacket merits any sort of special treatment. No matter.

So, there he is standing before me, expectant, keyed-up, and we mustn't disappoint him. "In your own good time, Mr er, er... – the somersault."

However, instead of getting on with it, he stands blinking up into my glowing light and "Yes," he says, "but... sir, if I could just know what the purpose of the... the... somersault is. You see..." Here I interrupt him.

"My dear Mr er, er... my dear chap, do you or do you not wish to be considered?"

At this, he thinks for a moment, repeats the word 'considered', finally understands what I mean... possibly – and possibly something of what my question implies – and nods, affirmatively.

"Oh... yes, sir..." he declares, a bit hesitantly, "I do... yes... I most certainly do..."

"Good! Then I'm sure you will appreciate that there are certain procedures laid down by our organisation, procedures designed to tell us quickly and efficiently who is and who is not likely to fulfil the requirements – you *do* see what I mean, Mr er, er... don't you?"

Somewhat chastened by my mild rebuke he nods his 'understanding', seems to shrug, perhaps resignedly, makes as if to crouch down, then at the last moment straightens up again. "It's just that… if you could just explain what…"

But at this further prevarication… provocation… I bang my fist down hard on the table, raising my voice noticeably, to observe: "Without your full co-operation we cannot proceed further and may as well terminate the proceedings now. If that is what you wish, Mr…"

That does the trick, of course! Without more ado down he goes, balancing on the balls of his feet, not quite making up his mind to launch himself forward.

"In your own good time", I say again, by way of encouragement – and to hurry him on, and "Go to it with all your might!" And finally he falls forward in a feeble attempt at what turns out to be not so much a forward roll as a sideways slither. Quite pathetic, with not the slightest trace of what they see as dignity… much less, grace. It's true enough, I have to acknowledge it; they don't really have any pre-eminence over all the other bits and pieces I dreamed up. I sigh heavily before pointing out the obvious: "Not exactly the best specimen of its type I've seen in my long experience of… Would you care to try again?"

"Is there no other way?" he asks, but I give him one of my steely looks. "There is no alternative", I say, emphatically, then wait, tapping my fingers loudly, rhythmically on the tray in front of me. Once again he crouches, hesitates, falls forward and this time cracks his forehead against the floor, having completely misjudged the height and the distance. And there he is on his knees, leaning far forward, rubbing his head with one hand and covering the back of it with the other, propped on one elbow.

'Truly, there is no profit for them at all under the sun', I reflect ruefully. If only I'd been a bit more patient, in the beginning… had had more practice at manipulating the shell, things might have turned out better. Too late now!

"Approximately how long have you been performing somersaults?" I inquire. At this he stops rubbing his head and straightens up until he's sitting back on his heels. He cranes round to look at me, and then explains what I already know to be the case: "But that's just the point, sir. It's what I was trying to say… I haven't. I don't. I don't have any call to. Not since they made us do them at school. And in any case…" But then he thinks better than to push his luck further…

In order to defuse the tension a little – not that I have anything against tension – I ring the bell again and we pause while yet again he watches with intense fascination the rehearsal of events on the other side. When this sequence has finished I write on the form – uttering the words quietly, though not too quietly, as I do so – "Lacking experience".

Surprisingly, instead of standing up, he crouches yet again and almost immediately lunges into something vaguely resembling a somersault and then, scrambling to his knees, yet again into the crouching position and over he goes again, improved, if still far from perfect. Laughing and panting hard he gets back into a kneeling position, just in front of me (appropriately, I think, though as yet he can't know that). "There sir, I did it. I

knew I could if I kept at it… Practice makes perfect…"
he adds, immodestly.

"Yes," I agree, "eventually… it does." And to this I
might add 'To every purpose there is time and
judgement, therefore the misery of man is great upon
him', but I don't, since that would be like salt in the
wounds to come. Yet, 'if the salt hath lost its savour…'
(can't remember how that one goes on…). Anyhow, by
way of encouragement I return to the form and say as
I amend it, "Lacking experience, but improving
steadily."

He looks pleased at that scattering of manna and I
let him savour it for a moment or two before I mention
the hoop.

"Hoop?" he says, still laughing at his little triumph,
yet becoming ever so slightly uneasy again. "Hoop, sir?
What hoop?"

I, for my part, feign surprise at his ignorance. "The
hoop", I say. "Everyone has to jump through the hoop.
Some many times, I might add. Didn't you know
that?"

Slowly he clambers back to his feet. "I'm sorry, sir, I don't think I have properly understood you." His face is grimy with dust and sweat, his hands black as infernal soot, and I can still see the red weal on his forehead where he'd hit the floor.

Things are shaping up nicely, and I am well pleased. "You don't understand?" I say, and he shakes his head slowly, clearly still trying to fathom it all out. "You will," I reassure him, "you most certainly will. In the fullness of time." At this he nods again, though with more than a little doubt still in his eyes. "For this," I suggest, trying to sound helpful, "it might be a good idea if you were to remove your shirt and your trousers, otherwise you will be far too restricted in your movements."

Curiously, his sense of triumph seems to have evaporated. "You mean," he says, as if trying to clarify matters aloud, "I have to jump through a hoop?"

"That is correct," I answer, wearing one of my more benign smiles, "but first you must prepare yourself... your shirt... your trousers...", and I nod meaningfully, beginning to feel a bit impatient now with the whole business. I've been through it all countless times before. And yet…

He starts to unbutton his shirt, then the front of his trousers, but suddenly bethinking himself he looks round furtively to make sure we are still alone – as if it mattered! Better men than he have danced naked before… me, before now…! Satisfied, he pulls off his shirt then drops his trousers, stepping out of them with some difficulty, tripping and staggering a few paces before falling heavily on his hands and knees.

I exhale sonorously.

I glance then at his puny body, its wispy bits of hair, his sagging belly, his thin, crooked legs. What a specimen! How on earth do they get themselves looking like this? What a thing is man! When I think what they start from…

No bright, gaudy, angelic butterfly here, that's for sure! The sooner the better, I ruminate, the sooner the better. For both our sakes.

I can feel my resolve beginning to harden and nod my head at his socks. "On second thoughts, Mr, er… Mr Court, isn't it? Your socks too… you may slip… otherwise."

And obediently, if wearily, he pulls off his socks, stands up a little unsteadily, rubbing his shin, then limps with his clothes over to the little table and deposits them neatly there, along with the rest. He pauses a moment or two, with his back towards me, before turning slowly, apparently intent on asking yet another question – and I sigh. He swallows, hard. "I should be much obliged, sir…" he begins, then falters, so obviously set on not giving offence, on not risking being cast out. "That is, sir, I was just wondering… about the hoop you mentioned… well, what is its purpose? – if you don't mind me asking…"

"Its purpose," I say loudly, "is for jumping through."

He thinks about this a while then decides he isn't sure that my answer has told him what he wants to know – if indeed he knows what it is he wants to know – which I very much doubt.

"I see, sir..." he says with suitable, habitual deference, "but why is that?" he adds, trying to draw me, yet at the same time trying to keep his patience, and presumably mine.

"Why?" I echo, then I fall silent for a moment or two, going through the wearisome charade of being deep in thought, of treating his question with the utmost respect, seriousness – they like to believe they're being taken seriously. Then slowly, I lean forward, and prompted by this he takes a couple of steps in my direction, ready to receive my considered answer.

When I judge the moment to be just right I deliver my judgement. "Because it is a hoop", I say emphatically, and with a finality that is absolute. He looks quite bewildered but decides not to pursue the question further, crushed by the simple mechanisms of Authority.

'Marvel not at the matter,' I reflect, 'for he that is higher than the highest regardeth.' I let the moment drift into silence, to let him cogitate on this... his latest failure to penetrate the seeming carapace of the world's mysteries, floundering as ever, slithering down the slippery slope of language, always trying to fathom the word.

When I judge the time sufficient, I bring him back to present unrealities. "Well now, Mr Shorthouse, you are ready for the hoop…" 'and the broken bowl, the pitcher broken at the fountain, the wheel broken at the cistern, the dust that returns as it was…' I might have added. "However, we shall of course require a little assistance", whereupon I press the button which sounds a buzzer. The sharpness of it makes him start and I can see he is trembling all over. Perhaps it's the cold, though mixed with a little fear, I should think… hope… yet not sufficient, I realise, to prevent him from making yet another of his feeble protests.

"You mean somebody else is coming? But you can't… you mustn't… let anyone see me like this. It would be a…"

"Can't? Mustn't?" I echo reprovingly. "But Mr Nort… I thought we had already dealt with these objections. I thought I had made it clear… There are certain procedures… certain inflexible laws in the nature of things – as I was at pains to explain earlier, and yes, I know, as you are at pains to discover now – and they cannot, must not, be transgressed…"

Before he can say anything else the door opens and in comes Miss Smith, carrying the paper-covered hoop in one hand and her usual ringmaster's whip in the other. On these occasions, her attire is very fetching, I always think – certainly, the supplicants seem to find it so – a top hat, a ringmaster's red coat tastefully unbuttoned almost to the waist, black fish-net stockings (as befits a fisher of men) and black high-heeled shoes, and apart from the sculpted makeup, that… is all, I like to think. Colourful though this attire is, I fancy it is more what she is not wearing than what she is that *their* fancy fixes on. It is undoubtedly so at our present interview, for to my surprise (and his utter confusion) I see him begin to rise to the occasion, and immediately, he claps his cupped hands over the front of his pants, quite distraught. Of course, as he well knows, 'there is a time for… everything', as one of my ad men put it… but this is decidedly not it.

"As you can see, Mr Mort, we practise a wholly transparent equality of the sexes here. We are an equal opportunities employer, after all…" And to prolong his moment of mortification a little further, I ring the bell beyond the partition and we all three watch as the routine procedure is completed, though with our Mr Tort struggling uncomfortably with his growing concern… When everything has returned to 'normal' on the other side, I gently remind him – and Miss Smith – about the hoop, lest he forget he is 'ensnared in an evil time', such as falls suddenly upon them at any time.

Miss Smith is very theatrically minded, and she flourishes both the whip and the hoop most… provocatively, rather like the matador with his bull. But as he still stands stock still, clutching his… excrescence, she begins to crack the whip, and that startles him… though he still doesn't show any signs of moving. So, a little impatiently – I sense – though with admirable dexterity, she flicks the whip so that it catches him lightly, though sharply, across his bare shoulder. And this not only elicits a sudden cry of pain… and maybe outrage… for who can rightly know what they mean…? but seems to galvanise him into action.

He hurls himself forward, bellowing loudly, whether at the hoop or at Miss Smith I cannot be sure; she, however, takes the necessary evasive action and thrusts the hoop forward so that he crashes into it, wrenching it from her hands, and ends up sprawling, as ever, in the dirt, his torso stuck in the broken hoop.

'Woe to him that is alone when he falls!', as they maintain I said at some time in the past. Can't remember, really… They're nothing but dust though. Just dust.

 So why do I go to all this trouble? Why?

And he lies there making strange animal sounds, growling almost, or maybe it is just his way of sobbing; difficult to know, really. Still, his performance is clearly and inexorably determining the outcome, for what can one do when ineptitude in all things is the sum total of a man's achievement? 'By their deeds ye shall know them' – that's one of mine… I think. Anyhow, I let him lie there, making his moaning sounds, his snuffling sounds, for quite some time because I want him to savour the enormity of it all, and there is nothing quite like silence or emptiness for echoing back their essential aloneness… their powerlessness… to them.

In all of this, Miss Smith is, as ever, quite splendid. It is undoubtedly her finest role. She stands astride him, arms akimbo, the whip still firmly held in her right hand, and with her top hat at a raffish angle. I really must remember to compliment her on her performance at some more appropriate moment… If only I could find time…

At last, Mr Crossly begins to stir, to return to us. He lifts his head and looks up in the direction of my blinding light. By this time his face is streaked with grime and blood, and his body is bruised, and I can see he is sorely afflicted. In trying to pull himself to his knees, his shoulders come in contact with Miss Smith's shapely thighs, and he stops moving, fixing his eyes on her left foot (or thereabouts), then after a moment or two's hesitation he tentatively reaches out a hand and strokes her ankle and her calf, but momentarily, barely touching her; one might almost believe, wistfully, withdrawing his hand slowly, watching it return to him, and afterwards looking back and upwards over his shoulder, to be met with the tip of her whip on his forehead, gently but firmly suggesting he return to his former prostration; which, of course, he does.

I fill in the penultimate section of the form, speaking the words aloud, even as I write them: 'Ill at ease; a square peg in a round hole.' But then, with forced cheerfulness, I encourage him to complete the physical part of the interview. As I expect, he shows definite signs of reluctance, shaking his head from side to side, and repeating, seemingly endlessly, "oh no, no, no, no, no…" – so negative about *everything*, this one!

It is time to remind him of where he is and why he is here. "Mr Crossman," I say sternly, "we have come this far, there remains but a little way to run." By now I feel very strongly indeed that there can be no perverting judgement or justice and the hour is almost at hand.

He sighs then and, with obvious discomfort, maybe even pain, begins once more the laborious business of rising to his knees. Miss Smith steps back a couple of paces and stands behind him. Steadying himself on his hands, he turns his face towards me: "Please sir, could I not ...?", and he breaks off, shaking his head again.

It is easy to despise them.

"Please sir, it's obvious... by now... that I'm not... quite... what you were looking for, that I'm not the right... material – whatever the position is. I thought it was something else, something... different. Could I not just put my clothes back on and leave, go back home, forget the whole thing?"

Miss Smith raises her arm high and brings the singing whip down hard across his back and shoulders and he shrieks with the pain of it. It is true indeed that 'in much wisdom is much grief and whoever increases wisdom increases grief also'. Coming so late in this case, what would it profit him?

"You have your answer, Mr Crossby. You see, it is not quite as simple as you imagine… You cannot waste our time like this… forever; dropping in and out as the whim takes you. The decision, I'm afraid, is no longer yours. The time for that is now past. There are certain procedures we cannot ignore, much less diverge from. Do you follow me?"

He nods submissively. "What must I do?" he then asks, looking straight ahead, seeking neither Miss Smith nor myself. 'To every purpose,' I am thinking again, 'there is time and judgement.'

"That's better", I comment, adjusting my tone a little, once more. "The final aptitude test… We need to see whether or not you are capable of a balanced approach, of not straying from the straight and narrow way, of keeping your head… up… under pressure. Look! There now, do you understand?"

"Understand?" he repeats. Then again, "understand?" He moves his head from side to side. "I think I shall never understand. It's all too… too… ridiculous to understand", and he goes on shaking his head, ruefully.

I wasn't altogether sure what he meant and, I must admit, I felt a bit offended … But, time was getting on and it was time it was ended.

"Right then, Miss Smith, the tightrope…" She nods but seeing no response from the supplicant, flicks the whip once more across his shoulders. The man winces but makes no complaint, slowly pushing himself up into a standing position where, however, he sways unsteadily from side to side. With her whip, Miss Smith points to the far corner of the room, near to the partition. He nods and shuffles slowly towards it, with Miss Smith behind him, cracking her whip explosively, rhythmically. Without waiting to be told, he mounts the brief ladder leading to the little platform and, spreading his arms wide, stands there, poised, preparing to step off onto the taut wire, the narrow way, the void…

Yes. There is something almost… admirable about the way he faces up to this last test. Miss Smith slips off her red coat, lays aside her whip and climbs the ladder at the opposite end, where she stands and beckons to him with a wave, smiling a fetching smile, her hips, her breasts swaying rhythmically.

On these occasions, I always think, she is quite magnificent.

Gingerly, he slides his front foot out onto the wire, testing it, sliding his foot back and forth, almost… expertly, as if he were going to finish in style.

I ring the bell beyond the partition but this time… as of course they must, the players crowded to the glass, their grotesque faces, their flattened noses, pressed against it, silently cheering him on.

I'm not sure whether he even noticed them, so absorbed was he with his own anticipated actions, still – for all I know – trying to impress, to win my approval and the ultimate prize – whatever he imagined it to be.

Miss Smith slid her foot out onto the wire, then drew it back, then out again, almost as if she were contemplating meeting him half way, but beckoning encouragingly all the while. I think it was this that spurred him at the last into his final action 'The woman-soul draws us, upward and on'. Did I say that…

or was it… what's his name, Shake… Shake…? Can't honestly remember – not that it matters overmuch, not now we come to the crossways… the crux of the matter. Anyhow, with arms spread wide, he slides out onto the wire, balancing, balancing, then brings his back foot round and forward… but that's as far as he gets. So near… yet, so far. He misses his footing and pitches headlong down, catching his shoulder on the wire as he falls so that it turns him over. There is a loud crack as he hits the floor and once again, I have to recognise, Paradise has been lost.

Miss Smith stands looking down… a touch ruefully, shaking her head from side to side, with Mr Cross lying spread-eagled on his back, his mouth open, his eyes open; his *colloquio* plainly at an end.

I shrug helplessly, and smile at her, then ring the bell once more, and slowly the players make their way back to their places to resume their game.

Miss Smith, by this time well practised in all of our procedures, comes down the ladder, steps over the inert Cross, and begins tidying up. She goes over to the little table and starts sorting through the clothes the man had worn. We recycle what we can. Some she takes and puts them on hangers in the huge wardrobe along the back wall of the room, others she throws into the basket near the door. Then she picks up her red coat, dusts it down a little with the back of her hand, and puts it on. Almost as an afterthought, she picks up the whip and the broken hoop, adjusts her top hat, and comes towards me.

This bit I always appreciate! Clambering up on the rungs of my chair a little way, she stretches out her hand and flicks the switch of my desk light. I have this… urge, to reach out and… touch her. I often wish she would speak to me in this particular moment, or even smile. But she never does.

She goes to the door then and switches out the light before exiting, closing the door behind her, leaving me, as ever, in the dark.

CHECKMATE

Somewhere in that nowhere between sleep and waking she became aware of her arm; of the dull ache in her upper arm.

But there were other sensations too, urging her up towards consciousness. A desperate need for water and an equally desperate need to relieve herself. Then there was the coldness of her feet and legs and she tried unsuccessfully, scrabbling about with her hands, to adjust the cover and in the end was reduced to drawing her legs up under her body, half realising that the cover itself was neither long enough nor wide enough to embrace all. This awareness ushered in another, that of her nakedness.

Yet it was the ache in her arm and her bladder that goaded her most.

And finally, topping the misty rise, her memory yawning and stretching all ways at once, she began piecing together what had happened: the pre-arranged, fake kidnap by the students, for publicity, for rag week – and, of course, charity. It had somehow taken a wrong turning.

A scuffle. There had been a scuffle – all a part of the verisimilitude, she remembered thinking. Being bundled into a van and suspecting, too late, that it wasn't security at all, wasn't her trusties. Then there was the needle. And now she moved her hand to cover the sore spot on her arm, connecting with reality, vowing through clenched teeth that someone would pay for this outrage and no mistake.

For all these pressing discomforts and mental adjustments, she was still reluctant to open her eyes. This final act of revelation demanded a Herculean effort of her will, but it was some moments yet before she was able to make it.

Immediately, she saw that directly above her, set into the ceiling, was a huge lamp, though its light was so weak it barely penetrated the gloom about her. She sensed therefore, rather than saw, that the room she lay in was very large and that she was its only occupant. When her eyes had grown accustomed to the penumbra, she sat up, pulling the cover around her shoulders. Almost at once, however, the light began to intensify rapidly and its sudden burst forced her to close her eyes and begin the process of adjustment all over again. Blinking hard and shielding her face with her hand, she gradually began to take stock of her surroundings.

The room was indeed large, and empty. On two sides there were what looked like parallel wall bars, maybe three metres high. The walls and ceiling were uniformly cream in colour. The floor was of polished wood. This much she took in at a glance. Obviously a gymnasium; a school or sports hall, and for a fleeting moment she felt optimistic, her mind connecting again with the students. The forming thought was short-lived, however, for her nakedness, which her eyes came back to in the glare of the light above her, belied that possibility; surely... they wouldn't dare. They wouldn't dare make her suffer such indignity, not even for publicity; not even for charity.

Looking down now she saw she had been lying on a striped mattress which was none too clean. She noticed several suspicious looking stains and her lip curled in disgust. The mattress was set in the middle of the room and with this realisation she suddenly felt extremely vulnerable and pulled the cover more tightly about her. This action, though it protected the upper part of her body, quite exposed her from the navel downwards, and she began tugging it down once more. Try though she may, she was unable to satisfy her own sense of propriety, and in her mounting frustration and anger she found herself – absurdly – trying to decide whether to give priority to her top half or her bottom half when she eventually stood up. And stand she must for her groaning bladder demanded she reach a bathroom quickly. And the ache in her arm persisted.

Once on her feet, though feeling quite unsteady, dizzy even, she turned slowly round towards the door she felt sure must be behind her. To her immense relief, her eyes lighted not on a door but a toilet, in the corner of the room, and she shuffled towards it, pulling the cover first up then down, then up again, with her left hand, while trying at the same time to keep it closed at the front of her body, with her right. She raised the lid and, to her disgust, found that the inside of the pan was caked with excrement. Snorting in anger, she pressed the flush which, though it worked, made little difference.

Though conscious of her rising nausea she knew there was no alternative but to sit, or rather, hover, and her immediate sense of relief hustled away all other thoughts and sensations. From her more elevated position, meticulously, minutely, her cold eyes surveyed the room, seeking the door, yet strangely, failing to locate it. A sudden noise away to her left caused her to turn sharply, and it was then she caught sight of what looked like a jug standing in a distant corner. So large was it she could not understand how she could not have seen it before. She would go and inspect not just the jug but the rest of the bare room. She looked round for a toilet roll but found none although there were three or four squares of newspaper on the floor to her right. Again a surge of disgust almost choked her, but there was no alternative, and reaching down she took hold of one of the sheets. She was startled to find it featured a picture of her. She snarled in her anger, dropped it and took up another, and this too, she soon discovered, bore her image together with that of the smiling Home Secretary. The remaining three sheets were similarly all pictures of her smiling or finger-wagging self.

Indignity was deliberately being heaped on indignity. Socialists! Communists! Scum!

It was while seeking to resolve this new dilemma that she caught sight of what looked like a surveillance camera high on the wall above her, perhaps because its red light had moved or flickered. And then it struck her that her every action was being watched, perhaps even filmed. Looking round in something like panic she saw that there were another seven or eight of them and all appeared to be pointing in her direction. She froze where she half-stood, the Home Secretary grinning smugly up into her face. Her sense of position, of status, of her high office was in direct conflict with fundamental human needs she had never questioned before, never needed to question. Her mind was like an embattled army, surging forward here, falling back there, thrusting and parrying, ducking and weaving, until at last dignity won the day and, with calm, measured precision, she replaced the Home Secretary (and herself) in the corner. Then, clutching the cover about her, she stood, flushed the toilet, closed the lid and stepped away, contempt remoulding her face – or maybe it was the moist discomfort of her thighs.

Her instinct – or perhaps it was the sense of her own towering importance that had grown about her like a second skin – dictated she stand to her full height as she moved off on her tour of inspection. Yet her somewhat bizarre, wholly inappropriate attire suggested otherwise. Paradoxically, the *realpolitik* of personal dignity drew her in and down, so that she found she was shuffling, almost bent double, to protect herself from those prying red eyes.

She knelt down beside the jug in the corner. It was half full of clear liquid, most probably water, but she remembered the needle and would take no chances, despite the raging thirst urging her to pick it up and drain it. Her iron will held steady and she smiled a superior smile of satisfaction, then, bethinking herself, she turned and repeated it more broadly, contumeliously, for the cameras. Her academic training came into its own – the power and certainty of science; she looked carefully, she smelt, she dipped her finger, waited a moment or two then allowed the tip of her tongue to touch the droplet still hanging on the tip of her finger. She knew there were other more reliable tests she could have applied, of course, but in these circumstances… and she lunged at the jug, almost upsetting it, seized it with both hands and jerked it up towards her lips, spilling the water in and around her mouth and onto her breasts in her haste to eviscerate the parchedness that seemed suddenly to be invading her whole body.

Only when it was empty did she remember the dignity and caution of a few moments before; but alas, too late, for her dignity – like the coverlet on the floor – had slipped lamentably, and on this occasion "they" had undoubtedly won their point. Steadying herself, she jerked the hateful piece of cloth up over her wet breasts, and with the difficulty these tricky manoeuvres imposed, somehow got to her feet.

But what was that attached to the wall-bars over there? And she shuffled stiffly across for a closer inspection. She blanched with horror as she gazed. Manacles, at shoulder height, and another pair intended to secure her – no, no, don't be ridiculous – to secure someone, yes someone, anyone, by the ankles. And the red smears on the wall behind them … But if these silent threats pressed on her fear, this was now greatly exacerbated by the sight of a heavy bull whip that hung neatly coiled just to her right. Reaching out, she tried to take hold of it, with some half-notion of arming herself against whatever eventuality … but alas! She was frustrated to find it was held fast by some locking device that would not yield, however much she yanked and twisted. Then yet again, too late, she saw that her cover had slipped away and lay once more on the floor around her ankles. With one arm swung across her breasts and the other making a last stand atop the knoll before the citadel of her modesty, she bent to retrieve it, all the while glaring defiance at the nearest of the cameras. "They" would not grind her down. No surrender! No surrender!

Secure once more – as secure, that is, as her abruptly straitened circumstances would allow – she set off in search of whatever other revelations her prison might offer, and of course, more specifically, in search of the way out and an end to all this nonsense. Yet all too soon, she had completed her circuit of the room and, to her utter amazement, had found nothing other than a few slogans daubed on the walls: 'On your bike!', 'Where there is suffering let me bring…' Insulting! Despicable! But certainly nothing resembling a door. She tapped the walls in various places, both high and low, for some suggestion of hollowness, but detected nothing. Here and there, she stamped her feet – and not only in the interests of detection – but to no avail. To all intents and purposes, the room was completely sealed.

With this realisation came the new suspicion that there might not be any supply of air and that her every exertion was perhaps using up whatever little remained. Was this prison then even worse than that, nothing less than the place of her immolation? But no, "they" wouldn't dare, whoever "they" were. No. No.

But this certainty, born of outrage, was short-lived, undermined by the memory of what had happened to that little Italian fellow, what was his name? Their Prime Minister. No more than what? Twenty, thirty years ago, was it? All the fault of the damnable sixties! No longer any respect for authority and position, no sense of the proper order of things. Try as they may, she and her colleagues had failed conspicuously to roll back the pernicious attitudes that had emerged during that most anathematised of all decades – and was not her present predicament yet one further demonstration of that incontrovertible truth? Her face twisted in anger and disgust.

With this galling problem gnawing at her pride – not to mention her possibly diminishing supply of oxygen – she returned to the mattress and sat down to wait, since there was nothing at all she could do to alleviate her situation. And she rubbed her sore arm, hoping it wasn't infected…

The next move, she realised, must necessarily come from "them". And she waited. Boredom flopped down beside her. She yawned in his face. And he yawned back. And again, with increasing frequency and volubility.

Struggle though she may, summoning up all her powers of concentration and her much-vaunted will in the interests of dignity, her eyelids drooped, nevertheless, and her head jerked forward. "Whatever would Winston have done in these circumstances? Or Margaret, of blessed memory?" she found herself wondering. She sank down onto one elbow, then, hardly aware of what she was doing, slowly lowered herself to lie full stretch and slipped into an uneasy doze. Uneasy not just because of all the uncertainties but because the water she had gulped down so voraciously was already beginning to make its presence felt, treacherously conspiring with those forces for evil without, to betray her and her unshakeable convictions, yet again.

She woke with a start, sure there had been a noise – or had she dreamt it? And she jerked bolt upright. But the sight of her ample bosom reminded her once more of the ongoing problem of… of, well, economy, she supposed, for she was exposed to the cameras yet again in all her nakedness. And again she struggled with the inadequacy of that piece of cloth.

How long had she slept, she wondered? There was no way of knowing.

Then she recalled the sound that had wakened her and looked around to see if anything was different.

Nothing that she could see. Carefully, she knelt and, shielding herself as best she could from the cameras, staggered to her feet. But she was mistaken. Over by where the jug still stood there was something else.

As she neared Jug Corner she realised, with disappointment, that it was only two or three bits of paper. Disappointment, yes, because hadn't she been hoping it would be something to eat? She had to admit it. She had. She was ravenously hungry. But I won't demean myself. Won't ask. Won't beg. Bastards! The jug was still empty. Bastards! Hunger, thirst, lack of air … And the ache in her arm. How could human beings be so callous? Filth! Dregs of humanity!

Taking up the bits of paper she saw that two of them were glossy advertising flyers, while the third, evidently torn from an exercise book, had scrawled upon it just two words, "Remember Cancoun?" Puzzled, she limped uncomfortably back towards the toilet and sat down. Of course she remembered Cancoun! Interminable talk about the Third World and its problems (all of them self-compounded), but it had had its memorable side too: excellent facilities and service, breathtaking scenery, and a bewildering array of exotic foods... but surprisingly, the Mexicans had certainly known how to entertain their all-important guests, just the right balance between deference and dignity... And yes, Margaret had been so gracious, so kind, and maybe Cancoun had been the moment in which her star had begun to rise. Was that what "they" meant, perhaps?

Emerging from the memory she wondered why "they" had asked her the question. Strange minds. Twisted. And she turned her attention to the flyers. One of them was advertising bed linen at sale prices – huge savings! And the other, lingerie, though from what she saw of it, hardly the sort of thing she would look twice at! Still, she reflected with some pride, both were testimony of the booming economy – and whose doing was that? She could certainly use some of the bedding though, and the underwear – if it had been half decent (which it clearly wasn't!). And consciousness of bed linen jolted her back to the present. Her cover – she didn't have it. She must have dropped it. And sure enough, there it was, in a heap at Jug Corner. Keeping up appearances was proving to be something of a strain, a nagging worry. Like the pain in her arm.

Ignoring the cameras, she marched to the corner and, as she picked up the cloth she saw there was yet another piece of paper beneath it. "I must have dropped it, first time... or just not noticed it." She started to read it as she turned away. An order form. An order form! Bedding and Lingerie! What sort of game were they playing with her? Dropping the cover absent-mindedly on the mattress, she scrutinised the leaflets more closely. Cheap, shoddy stuff... but better than nothing... in the circumstances... I'll have two sheets and two blankets – there don't seem to be any duvets. Really! And a couple of pillows. And pillowcases. Then what about the other stuff?

It was hard to know which made her blush the more – illustrations or captions. 'Slinky knicks' were decidedly not her style, nor crotchless tights...

Crotchless tights? How absurd! What use were they! Nor silky thongs… nor the transparent French… things… But there appeared to be nothing else, certainly nothing sensible. If only there were someone to communicate with she could begin to explain *her* requirements – which were not served at all by the present choices.

"Hello!" she shouted; the word echoed around the room, then fell exhausted beside her.

She tried again. "Hello! Is there anyone there?"

And the silence echoed back.

And, however reluctantly, she placed her order, or would have – and she could not resist a contemptuous sneer at the realisation – had she had a pen with which to do so. She made writing gestures at the camera; saucily it winked its red eye. And she waited. And nothing happened. And again, as she waited, sleep stole upon her and laid her low.

She had a curious dream in which she was patrolling what looked like the cages of battery hens, though they were much larger, and occasionally a head would protrude from one of them and when it did, she hurried towards it and yanked the hatch down, trapping the head outside, its tongue lolling, its red eyes goggling. All of them were men she knew – the Home Secretary was among them – and with each she bade them say 'please' and when they failed to do so she leaned heavily on the hatch, reminding them, in Margaret's famous phrase, 'there is no alternative…'

When she awoke the light had all but gone and, once again, she reluctantly dragged herself off to the loo, and as she went she became aware that the cameras were all moving with her, focusing on her. As she sat there, contemplating her predicament, she became sharply aware of how hungry she was. She rose and, without any qualms, wiped herself meticulously on the Home Secretary – who had singularly failed to protect her – pulled the cursed cloth about her, and felt her way along the bars to the corner where the jug was… or, had been… Now it was no longer there but in its place there were other things… a torch that shed a feeble light (its batteries were obviously near to failing – the fools!), a red biro, a booklet of some description and… among various papers, a menu. What on earth did they think they were playing at? She gathered everything up as best she could and carried it all over to her island home, dropping them on it as soon as she got there. Then in a flash it came to her: all she need do was drag the mattress over to one of the walls and half the cameras would no longer be able to see her. But the rest would. So what was the point…?

Point or not, that was what she did, with a vague sense of triumph; when your back's to the wall it's best to… have your back to the wall… tugging at her mind. And strangely, she felt better, if not quite secure then certainly less vulnerable. And with this momentary lifting of her spirits she settled down to read, as best she could, by the feeble light of the flickering torch, the various bits of paper that her captors had left her.

'Is it really true that there is no such thing as bad publicity?' (she read)

'The oxygen of publicity may be the only oxygen you'll ever get...' (she read)

'Protect and survive!' – and attached to it a publicity leaflet – 'Sturdy oak tables, half price, £59.99 (while stocks last)...'

Tears came into her eyes and she was glad of the veil of near-darkness in that moment.

She picked up the menu, but it turned out to be no menu at all, rather a price list which admittedly contained a number of foods, but she couldn't see the point of it... unless... and instinctively, she reached for her handbag, but it wasn't there... so she had no means of paying, if that was indeed their intention... And again, crestfallen, the tears once again filled her eyes and began to roll down her cheeks...

She turned now to the final item, blinking through the tears, squinting in the feeble light, and with difficulty she gradually came to the realisation that it was some sort of paying-out book, for every page was identical in form, except that the dates, hand-written in the top, left-hand corner, were all a week later than the last, and there were twenty of them in all, all filled in for the identical amount of £87.49... Aghast, she realised that the slips were suggesting her captivity was envisaged for at least five months, perhaps even longer... while the odd amount... there was something familiar about it, though she couldn't in that moment say what... Pinned to the very last page she found a scrap of paper which said very simply... what she herself had said (very simply), in a speech, not two weeks before: 'The thrifty housewife will always manage, however small her budget.'

She picked up the discarded price list and considered her options. Moet & Chandon was definitely out of the question; as was the Islay single malt... and when it came to actual food well, even game pies would gobble up her meagre allowance long before a week was out... and as she moved through the list the prices of things gradually reduced, but the calculator in her head was telling her that even modest things like T-bone steaks or turbot or quails' eggs were way beyond her budget... All right! She would show them. She would lead by example… though in the end, when she had settled for a beef-burger and 'hand-cut chips' and a mug of tea, and realised that that had already taken up a tenth of what she presumed was her weekly allowance, she did vaguely wonder what that example would amount to. And for whom.

She marked her choices, went over to the corner where the hatch or whatever it was, was situated, and left them there together with her first paying out slip… A silly game they insisted on playing. All right, she would humour them!

Some time later, she heard the hatch open, and by now desperate to eat, she scurried over in anticipation of the meal she had ordered, only to find a sealed envelope, addressed to her. Back she traipsed with it to her refuge, turned on the torch, which by this time was flickering hysterically, tore open the envelope and found a three-and-a-half page long, jargon-ridden communication which purported to be from the State Pensions' Department and which informed her (once she had more or less mastered its arcane terminology) that pensions could only be paid out on the proper day, which was Tuesday. As today was Wednesday nothing could be done until next week... however, a loan could be arranged immediately, at a 'competitive rate of interest (18%)'... She felt the blood draining from her and she was distinctly faint, as well as very cold. This was monstrous! It was inhuman... and tearing a piece off the letter she began to write furiously, a strongly-worded protest, and when it was finished she strode off to the letter box and left it there. Halfway back to her mattress the torch finally gave out and she was left floundering in the dark.

In those moments after the light went out the blackness was total. It seemed to have both mass and volume, became an impenetrable undergrowth, and she froze in her sudden terror. The space about her, which her mind and memory told her was large, yes, but entirely encompassed, nevertheless was now transmogrified into something endless, stretching away towards infinity in all directions, and its immensity crushed her. She began to sob, silently at first, but the sense of hopelessness that gripped her urged her towards utterance so that she broke through the barrier of silence and the sound of her own choking sobs was in some inexplicable way reassuring. She stood there hoping for some adjustment of her eyes, some glimmer of light, and she was afraid to take a step in any direction for the darkness was full of terror, but she knew also that if she remained where she was, rooted to that spot, she would be trapped forever by those same, unfathomable fears. And her choking sobs blundered out into articulation: "Our Father, Who art in Heaven…" and it shocked her that the long-unrehearsed words came so easily to her mouth, but she hustled the words along none the less, desperate to reach the plea 'and deliver us from evil' in the primitive half-conviction that it was vital to her survival, the key that would unlock the door to her own, seemingly unlikely, continuation in… and she shuddered, dismissing the rest of that unthinkable thought.

And suddenly time resumed.

A sharp grating sound, then another, and a faint glow coming from behind caused her momentarily to abandon all caution and she spun round, fearful lest those frail co-ordinates that told her she was not alone, after all, in all this vastness, should disappear as randomly as they had come. Of course, it was the hatch... or whatever it was... opening and shutting, of course, that was it, but that moment of rationality was immediately supplanted by a further surge of emotion as her mind battened down on the tiny red glow coming from, directing her towards, the corner. And she scurried towards it, clutching her cloth about her.

The jug had reappeared. And there was another envelope.

She knelt down close to the minute glow of the bedside light... one of those night-light things they sell for children who are afraid of the dark. Her own two had never been allowed them... and she lifted the unsealed flap of the envelope. Inside it she found a small piece of paper blandly informing her:

'We regret that the office is now closed. Office hours are between 9.30am and 7.30pm. We apologise for any inconvenience.'

And there she was, shrieking at the hatch, "For God's sake, stop all this tomfoolery and get me something to eat, at once!"

But the silence closed immediately around her last word and settled all about her. She groaned her resignation to a world beyond her control, pushed herself off her knees with some difficulty, picked up the full, heavy jug and the little light and set off in the intuited direction of Mattress Promontory, utterly cowed and depressed. Her arm was aching again and she was very cold. She clung to the mattress and tried to arrange the cloth tightly about her, wedging it beneath her body where she lay, but it kept slipping out and what little heat had accumulated was dissipated in seconds. She passed an exceedingly uncomfortable night, if night it was, sleeping only fitfully, her dreaming continuous but quite uncoordinated.

Waking with a start, she sat bolt upright in the half light, not at first comprehending anything, but then it all swept in upon her, and she knew. Her mouth was dry, her bones ached with the cold and she felt nauseous from hunger. She splashed a little water from the jug into her mouth but that had the effect of making her need the loo at once and she clambered unsteadily to her feet and lurched away across the room. Astride the filthy bowl she had the idea she would visit the corner where the hatch was, as soon as she had finished, on the off chance something had been left for her there, in the night.

As she drew close, she saw there was yet another envelope, but nothing else, and her sense of disappointment was acute. She tore the envelope open and read:

'We trust you had a comfortable night – as comfortable as any spent by the many homeless beggars occupying shop doorways, park benches and the subways of the capital. You may even have noticed them, and possibly even wondered how they came to be there; though possibly not.'

Her eyes were brimming with tears, though certainly not for the plight of the homeless, who had only themselves to blame... the spineless underclass, the riff-raff, expecting to live off government hand-outs... but cold and hunger brought her sharply back to the present moment and her own predicament. The hunger was in "their" hands and she must bear that but the cold... that she could do something about, she would show them... and screwing the envelope and its message up into a ball she flung it down, contemptuously, and once she had reached her mattress refuge she began first of all to jump up and down, then at the same time to swing her full-stretched arms out and around her body... She'd always been a high achiever in the gym at school... But then she became aware of her bouncing breasts and the ridiculous spectacle she would be presenting to the watching cameras – and sure enough, they were all pointing her way – and she stopped at once, panting hard from the unaccustomed exertion. What heat she had generated was quickly lost and now she was trembling with cold. She sank down on the mattress, pulled the cloth tight about her and once again gave way to tears. "Oh, please!" she howled, "please show me some kindness."

The dreary hours crawled by, and having no means of measuring time she lost all sense of it. Sometimes the lamp at the centre of the room was bursting with light, at others it showed barely a glimmer, but there was no pattern to it, no logic that she could see. And the silence pressed down on her, broken only occasionally by her own exasperated cries, or her tears, or the sound of the hatch on which, she soon realised, her whole being was now centred. It brought hope or added frustration or despair, but at least gave her a sense of momentary change in this otherwise entirely static, utterly isolated, existence.

The bedding gradually arrived. Not the crisp, clean, white sheets she distinctly remembered from the advertisement, but grubby, used, soiled articles. First a smelly blanket and foul-looking, striped pillow that seemed as though it had spent much of its recent life at a landfill site; these accompanied by a cover note informing her that 'sheets and pillow cases are temporarily out of stock'. She howled in derision and despair, but the cold soon forced her to put aside her finer instincts, and she wrapped the coarse, dirty blanket around her.

Then her underwear arrived – clearly not what she had ordered, as far as she could tell in the half-light – and she had the greatest difficulty working out just how one should put these ridiculous next-to-nothings on – but at least these were new… she presumed. Somewhat later she found a sheet and a pillow case waiting for her, neither of them in any better state than the things received earlier. The food, when it came at long last, was at best tepid and had gone cold by the time she finished wolfing it down… And with each opening of the hatch she scuttled towards it, almost as though trying to reach it before its sound had died. And the light had a habit of being at the full for these excursions, though it rapidly dipped to penumbra for her return journeys.

It was when the financial details arrived in their sealed envelopes that her spirits sank to their lowest ebb yet. First the details of her 'loan' at 'just 18%'. Then the invoice for her bedding which, despite being on 'special offer' with a 'fifteen per cent discount', nevertheless took more than half the sum 'borrowed'. The bill for her meagre meal came to over nine pounds… and in her exasperation she sat and screamed abuse at the extortion, the arbitrariness, the unregulated prices against which she, a helpless captive, had no defence, no hope of redress…

And when she had once again achieved a measure of composure she calculated that, by the time their 'Wednesday' had come round, she would be hopelessly trapped in debt which, she realised, would quickly spiral out of control. There was no way she would be able to make ends meet. And not knowing what sanctions "they" would use against her she sank to new levels of anxiety and despair, utterly at "their" mercy. If only she could talk to them, to anyone, instead of being faced continually by this impersonality, absence, silence and inhumanity...

She woke suddenly, and sat up, but even as she did so she found she was wondering whether the waking was not really just a part of her dream. Was she dreaming? There was an eerie, flickering light all around her in the darkened cavern, the shadows shifting and darting, then subsiding, only to start again, and she became aware of an almost imperceptible whirring sound, though she could not pin-point where it was coming from. As her senses gathered about her, at last, she half-turned and at once realised she was about to see a film of some sort, projected onto the wall at the far end of the room. A film? And there it was, already stuttering its opening, mute message: 'Maximum Prophet Productions Ltd.' She turned fully round, her curiosity aroused.

Oh, my God! This was not entertainment... Her worst fears were being realised before her eyes: there she was, naked to the world, astride the filthy toilet, wiping herself (in zoomed-in close up) and obviously, purposely doing so on the newspaper portrait of the Home Secretary; now here she is struggling with that infernal piece of cloth; then again jumping up and down, her... flesh... bouncing, and with such a ridiculous look upon her face! And look, that silly, loping, crouching movement as she hurries over to the hatch door. And... oh, my God! Inspecting these idiotic knickers they have foisted on her, pulling them on, checking to see what they cover... and don't cover; but again, that look on her face... this is all so unfair, so... unjust.

No. Oh no! If they release this upon the world, and I'm sure they intend to... then there really is no way back... So that's it? But have they finished now with their humiliations or is there more to come?

She realises in that moment that whatever she does from now on, while still their captive, it will count for nothing in her political future. Her dignity is gone and without that her political career is at an end. She turns her back on the film and slides down under the bedclothes once more, closing her eyes, unwilling to look further at the shame to which she has been condemned.

Her debts mount as the days drag by. She is continually hungry, cold, tired and listless and slips gradually into depression, sitting on her mattress for hours on end, seeing no end, deserted by her former strength of mind and purpose and direction. And forever goaded by reminders of her past pronouncements which, even to her, now, in these circumstances, appear much more vacuous than vatic. She is reminded too that yes, the 'system' is heavily weighted against her, artificially, maliciously weighted against *her* by her tormentors, she knows that, but she sees too there is no way, even with the most determined will in the world, she can get herself out of this hole, this Hell not of her own making. But she is hardly alone in this predicament, they remind her, her tormentors; open your eyes wider, your mouth less... Look about you, see, learn.

An ice-cold blast striking her face like hail forces her to open her eyes. Her first instinct is to take refuge beneath the covers, in their fetid warmth, in the comfort of that so-familiar reek of her unwashed body. But after several moments of indecision she jerks upright, looking about her, seeking the source of this persistent glacial current.

When her eyes and mind at last co-ordinate she realises that in the corner, where the hatch should be, is a door standing slightly ajar; so that was it, and even as she watched it swung listlessly back and forth, the gap between door and jamb widening then narrowing continually by turns.

What could it mean? She watched without taking her eyes away for one moment, barely blinking even, more than half-convinced that in an instant it would slam shut. She must try and prevent it, at all costs.

Yet instead of rising and hurrying over to wedge it somehow, she clings to the mattress with both her clawed hands, then slips down under the covers and pulls them up over her head. She is panting hard, she realises, without really understanding why. She puts a hand to her breast and finds her heart is pounding. She chokes back a sob, feeling quite helpless, incapable of any action.

How long she stays like that is impossible to know for it had been time not air that had quit her prison cell, and with that flight the space all about her had become a vacuum. Eventually, she knows she must move, for the usual reason, but she keeps glancing at the still gently swinging door, suspicious of it, afraid even. She gathers up her blanket and wraps it around her as she totters to her feet, then steadying herself she backs away from the mattress and the door, towards the far corner. She sits down heavily on the filthy rim, the seat having worked loose then fallen off with a heavy clatter on the wooden floor, aeons ago, lying even now where it had fallen.

She sits there – like Elizabeth Porter, she thinks, and laughs out loud, beginning to sing a few bars of the song. But the sound startles her, the sound and the realisation that her voice is cracked and tuneless. She laughs again and stands up, carelessly wiping herself on the blanket.

And the door goes on swinging.

As it catches her attention once again she stumbles cautiously towards it, ready to turn back at the slightest hint of, of... of... she isn't sure what, but ready to turn... Reaching it, she stands watching its movement, fascinated, not at first comprehending how it can be swinging in both directions when the strong current of air is coming in only the one direction. But then she notices that the top hinges are missing and the weight of the door has buckled and partly torn away the lower ones, so that its movement is elliptical, something that had not been apparent at a distance. Suddenly, she thrusts out her hand and catches it on its next inward swing, and at the same time, the blanket slips away from her left shoulder and halfway down her body. But she stands holding the door, unaware or unconcerned, staring out through it, feeling the cold current on her exposed parts, a sensation of almost dizzying exhilaration. But she does not venture through it.

While her eyes are adjusting to the light of day, she finds she is looking across a wide corridor to another open door, wide open, fastened back, it seems, to the outer wall of the building. Beyond the door a broad expanse of crumbling concrete stretches away towards the remains of a low, crumbling brick wall, it too having its gateway, though the gates themselves were gone. And further still, wherever her eye travels, things are grimed and crumbling; there is a factory, its windows and doors boarded up for the most part, though here and there are broken windows, and gaping holes in its roof. It squats in squalid streets, with more boarded doors and windows, many more. A young girl and a small boy are playing with what looks like a metal hoop, taking turns at rolling it against the end wall of the factory, where it falls, each time, to be retrieved by whichever of the two had not rolled it. She watches, fascinated, waiting to see the point of the game, but that was it really, there was none other apparent. The streets… the figures… Yes, the matchstick men and women by… whoever it was… come to mind. What was he called? Maybe she has never known… she can't bring it to mind now, not that it matters… she has never bothered with such things… always more important things to think about.

Then withdrawing her longer gaze, she focuses now on what is nearest to her. It is a school building isn't it? Or it has been, for as she peers first left and then right along the corridor she realises that most of its windows are boarded up too, though in some cases the wooden planks have been ripped down and the windows smashed. Her sight now fully adjusted to her surroundings, she sees there is excrement dotted here and there, all the way down the corridor, and torn exercise books, discarded fast-food trays and their contents, and other disgusting things… and clearly, someone has at some time lit a fire for there is ash scattered about, and the flaking paintwork has been scorched from a whole section of the outer wall.

She swivels her eyes back towards the open door, and wonders what she can possibly do. Freedom of sorts beckons but a whole seething knot of emotions and sporadic thoughts and memories keep her riveted to the spot, still holding on to the elliptical door. Then she sees herself. To the left of the outer door there is a slim, full-length mirror. It is split apart, right down the middle, but is still miraculously, somehow or other, held in place. She stares at it, aghast, at her divided self, her sunken cheeks, her sunken breasts, her thin legs protruding from beneath the greasy blanket. How changed she looks. Unrecognisable almost, even to herself. So much of her has fallen away, down the fissure in the mirror, irretrievably, she fancies.

Sidling through the elliptical door she stands on the threshold and wearily averts her gaze, looking out once more at her policies' legacy; a sharp intake of breath; a hand straked across her misting eyes. She pulls the blanket up around her shoulders and holds it fast with both hands, above and below, at the front, but still cannot quite yet find the courage, or the will, or the effrontery maybe... to take that first step towards the other side of the corridor.

THE RISE (AND RISE) AND FALL OF GIANLUCA DELLE POZZA NERE

As the young man turned into Borgo de' Greci he glanced back over his shoulder. It wasn't that he expected to see anyone following him – it was all too recent for that – more an indication of his slight, and maybe increasing, uneasiness that, if he once allowed himself to consider its implications, it might even add up to a sense of guilt. But if it was indeed that, or something akin to it, tugging gently but insistently at the folds of his fashionable cloak, his thoughts, force-fed on imagination and ambition, raced far ahead of him, full of anticipation.

At first, he had found it well-nigh impossible to believe his good fortune, and in the possibilities – no more than that, mind you – which his colleague, nay, his friend, Collalto, had excitedly placed before him that very morning.

Neither of them found his employment in the Chancellery at all congenial to his spirits or his temperament, to say nothing of the different artistic ambitions each one of them harboured. It had been this distinct lack of enthusiasm that had brought them together, despite the long-running hostility that divided their families, since each, in his way, felt himself to be the victim of a tyrannical father whose ideas were as unreasonable as they were outmoded.

Collalto would gladly have given himself to music and to poetry but his father had insisted that he do something 'useful' with his intelligence and education, dismissing his protestations with a single swift toss of his hand unaccompanied by any word. A few days after this peremptory and wholly one-sided interview, Collalto was summoned yet again into his father's presence to be informed that a position had been found for him in the Second Chancellery and that he must betake himself there early on the following morning to present himself (and his father's somewhat grudging salutations) to the Secretary, Master Machiavelli.

With Gianluca (for that was the young man's name) it had been much the same story, except that there had been only one interview, not two, in which his father had told him bluntly that he would brook no dissent, that he had spoken that very afternoon with his old friend, Master Niccolò, and that the latter would expect him in his office in the Chancellery at eight of the clock on the morrow. "We'll put an end to this painting nonsense once and for all", he had added, before turning back to the papers littering his desk. Gianluca had stood there in bewilderment, not sure whether his audience was at an end, but as his father did not raise his head from the papers that seemed suddenly to have absorbed him so totally, he bowed unseen, turned on his heel and left the room, closing the heavy, double door quietly behind him. He had repaired at once to his chamber where in anger, as much as frustration and despair, he had given himself up to tears for the best part of an hour. That had been almost a year ago, and if such a fit of uncontrolled emotion had never been repeated, its underlying causes had remained, indeed, had intensified with each endless-seeming day as Master Niccolò's personal secretary. Days and days spent writing or transcribing the same dull matter amid spasms of yawning and a constant battle against heavy, drooping eyelids.

But now here he was, all of a sudden, walking rapidly along the long, straight street which, at its far end, opened out into the wide and populous piazza. Collalto had rushed into his room the moment Master Niccolò had returned to his own, to tell him what he had heard and to suggest that with just a modicum of courage and rather more of good sense, it might yet prove to be Gianluca's salvation.

At first, Gianluca had not quite caught the drift of his friend's speculation, perhaps because his delivery had been rushed and garbled, so excited was he. "This *Maestro* you speak of ..." he had begun, falteringly, "this *Maestro* from Venice. How did you come to hear of him?" And Collalto, clearly impatient that his friend had not yet grasped the real significance of his news, explained, again hurriedly, that the *Maestro* had rented rooms from his father, who had spoken of it at table the previous evening, adding – with more than a touch of disapproval in his voice – that the *Maestro* had vouchsafed his intention of painting a large, allegorical canvas whilst in the city, bearing the title *Gli sposati per l'amore* (Married for Love) – or some such nonsense – though in truth, it appeared, his father had barely paid heed to his words, rather more to the number of ducats he was offering. But the really important point was that the *Maestro* would be looking for models for his grand project – another thing his father had apparently mentioned. Here, Collalto had paused, his gaze intense, awaiting Gianluca's reaction, and when the latter had failed to respond he had almost screamed in his exasperation: "But can't you see? Can't you understand what I'm getting at? He needs models! Being a model would be one way of getting into conversation with him. You might be able to show him some of your own work. And who knows, one thing leads to another. He might even take you on as an apprentice. Isn't that how most great painters begin?"

At last, Gianluca saw the point. "You mean that I should offer myself as a model? But my dear Collalto, I have never... I mean... but yes, I see your... with just a little courage... Why not? Indeed, why not?" But it was only at that juncture that he had begun to think. How could he do it, tied down as he was every day at the Chancellery? His face clouded and he began to express his doubts, and his disappointment. Collalto, however, would have none of it. Perhaps something could be arranged for the afternoons when his duties at the office were completed. He could only try. He must. Besides, the opportunity of being taught by so great a master hardly came one's way every day. If he didn't seize the moment he would perhaps regret it for the rest of his life. And with such arguments Gianluca's mood gradually swung back towards optimism and he finally declared his intention of seeking out the *Maestro* that very afternoon. Collalto had thoughtfully brought the address with him, though he was not sure of the great man's name – unless it was Lorenzo. Yes, maybe that was it. Lorenzo. But surely, it would be enough to address him as *Maestro*?

So, here he was, elated yet uneasy, about to turn towards Via delle Vecchie Stinche from where, if Collalto had remembered correctly, it was but a few more steps to the side street in which the *Maestro* was lodged. And still he looked back nervously, aware of his father's certain displeasure should his visit be discovered, even if nothing were to come of it. If things were to turn out well, however, his fury would know no bounds. Yet, as if this were not trouble enough, he was also well aware of things Master Niccolò had warned against, among which, if his memory served him rightly, an explicit prohibition against entering into any other man's employ. Yet surely, this was different, it could not really be thought of as employment, not really. His spare time was his own and what he did with it was his own affair. The Chancellery did not own him... He was worrying needlessly... Of course he was. And yet, he looked back.

The door was finally opened by a small woman of indeterminate age, but of more calculable girth, dressed entirely in black. As he began to make his inquiry, she pulled the door wide open and beckoned him in with her other hand. A little taken-aback, Gianluca faltered, then he began again to explain why he was here, at the same time stepping inside. The woman, however, turned away, and bade him follow her with a further movement of her hand. He closed the door behind him then hurried after her down a long corridor towards a flight of steps at the far end. Still he tried to explain, but either she didn't hear him or simply ignored what he was saying. Hopefully, he thought, he might soon meet someone else who was a little less peremptory or a little less stupid, whichever was the case. Up the steps they went, a long, stiff climb which had even Gianluca panting by the time they came to the only door on the top landing. He saw that it was ajar as they approached, the woman presumably having left it so when she came down to answer his knocking. Once more she turned and waved him inside. As he entered, he was quite blinded by the sudden glare flooding into the mansard room from a large, open window, so much so that he was compelled to cover his eyes. He heard a low yet merry chuckle coming from somewhere across the room, but several moments passed before his sight was sufficiently restored for him to be able to see its author, a tall, thin man, whom he judged to be on the threshold of his middle years, standing with his back to the window, his elbows resting on the sill. The woman in black had disappeared but he then saw that another woman, with long black hair, was sitting in a low chair with her back towards him. Between the woman and the man at the window, there was a low table and another, higher chair, and at the nearer end of the table, a third chair. But what surprised him more than the lack of furniture and the stark simplicity of the little there was, was the fact that on the table stood a pewter tray with a wine flask and three goblets. Even before he spoke, the man was pouring wine into the goblets and handing them round, almost, it seemed, as if they had awaited his arrival.

The *Maestro* had resumed his stance before the open window. He drank a generous measure of wine then set his goblet on the sill beside him. "Well, young man, I imagine you are here to model for me. Am I right?" Gianluca nodded.

"You are already in employment, are you not?" Again, Gianluca nodded, though wondered vaguely how the *Maestro* had guessed this.

"Would that not then restrict your availability? You will know, I am sure, that I can only paint when the light allows. Fortunately, as the summer season is now upon us, that should prove less of a problem than it might otherwise be. What I have in mind would be eight, maybe as many as ten sittings in the middle part of the day. I cannot afford to pay generously, since coming here from Venice has already involved me in great expense. No more than three silver florins for each session." At this point he looked quizzically at Gianluca, clearly requiring some reaction to his words.

Since the amount was immaterial to him, Gianluca nodded his assent, then went on to explain that it would not be possible for him to arrive sooner than he had just now, though on Saturdays he would be free an hour earlier. The *Maestro* frowned and stroked his beard, then turned away to gaze out of the window. After a few moments' silence he turned again. "That could be rather inconvenient", he said. "I shall have other young men to see before I can come to a decision. If you are still interested, come back again at the same hour, in two days' time. Then I shall have decided."

This outcome was no less than, in his heart of hearts, Gianluca had expected, and yet his disappointment cut deep. To have his hopes raised and dashed in the span of but a few moments left him bewildered. But there was nothing he could say that might give him preferment; after all, the *Maestro* was merely interested in his physical being, and not at all in the passionate ambition that had really brought him hither. He rose to leave. The *Maestro*, however, motioned to him not to be so hasty, and he resumed his seat.

"What is this work you do that robs you of the best hours of the day and blackens the ends of your fingers?" Gianluca sighed, then briefly explained the nature of his duties at the Chancellery, leaving no doubt in a listener's mind as to his own attitude towards them. The *Maestro* nodded his understanding, smiling slightly as he did so – which Gianluca readily interpreted as sympathy for his plight. "Tedious in the extreme, I do not doubt", he added, as if to confirm the young man's surmise. "And yet," he went on, "necessary to the well-being of the commonwealth in these troublesome times – labours of a very (and here he paused, searching carefully for just the right expression)… of a very sensitive nature; one slip of the pen, one moment of inattention to detail, and the thoughts the Secretary or his superiors seek to convey are thwarted, distorted, and diplomacy goes by the board. A very responsible task is what you have described – if I have understood you aright." Gianluca realised he had never quite thought of what he did in that way, but he nodded, somewhat gravely. "Indeed," he agreed, "indeed it is." He leaned forward and reached for the goblet on the table before him, maintaining his air of seriousness, perhaps glimpsing in the two – the well-charged goblet and his assumed air of seriousness – a way of prolonging the interview to his advantage.

"Your correspondents must be many and varied," hazarded the *Maestro*, "important men from different lands, no doubt?"

"That is indeed so", Gianluca confirmed. "Why, only this morning, I was copying a letter – a very delicate letter – from His Excellency, Piero Soderini to no less a personage than His Holiness, Pope Julius." And then, perhaps with the intention of nourishing the seed which had already taken root in the *Maestro's* mind, he added, with just a touch of nonchalance, "but then, for me – as you say, 'in these troublesome times' – this is almost a daily occurrence."

A silence ensued in which each seemed to ponder Gianluca's words; the *Maestro* shaking his head pensively, Gianluca sipping at his wine in some satisfaction. Then the *Maestro* called them back to the moment. "Well, young man, perhaps we shall yet find the means of rescuing you from these heavy responsibilities you bear for the common good. As I say, I shall doubtless have others to see in the furtherance of my project, but if you have a mind to, return hither the day after tomorrow."

Gianluca smiled as he rose and assured the *Maestro* that he would with all his heart. He bowed deeply to the *Maestro* but then suddenly bethinking himself he felt he ought also to make some token recognition of the silent lady whom neither he nor the *Maestro* had thought to draw into their conversation. Someone of little account, no doubt, otherwise the *Maestro* would have introduced her, and yet common courtesy demanded it of him. He inclined his head in her direction, "By your leave, *signorina*", he said, softly, but either she did not hear, or chose to ignore him, so that he had to rescue himself from an awkward silence and withdraw, as he had entered, in some confusion.

As those final moments receded further into the past, he tended to dismiss them as mere aberration on his part, a miscalculation anyone could have made, anyone at all, while what really mattered was the overall impression he had left in the mind of the *Maestro*, and he had not the slightest doubt that that had been very, nay, extremely positive.

One can therefore imagine the turmoil into which he was further thrown when, on returning to the *Maestro's* lodging as arranged, he was informed that a choice had indeed been made but that it had not, alas!, fallen on him. Admittedly, the choice had been a difficult one. The *Maestro* had ruminated over it at some length but, finally, had decided in favour of another, equally personable young man, one with fewer pressing responsibilities to the world at large. Quite cast down he turned to leave, but as he reached the threshold the

Maestro, perhaps with the kindly intention of sweetening the bitter pill, asked him where he might be contacted should anything fall amiss with the agreement he had concluded. Gianluca thanked him for his solicitude, reminded him that he was to be found toiling daily in the Second Chancellery, secretary to Maestro Machiavelli, and went on his way, not quite comprehending how life could have betrayed him so cruelly.

If Gianluca had been restless in his occupation before these incidents, how much more so now when, like Orpheus, he had had salvation within his grasp, with the light shining before him, and yet somehow, quite inexplicably, everything had returned to dust. He was out of humour with all who crossed his path. He avoided his parents and siblings as much as he could, ate his meals in silence, betook himself uncommonly early to his chamber each night, yet could settle to nothing. He returned continually in memory to that first meeting and continually he remained convinced that there had been nothing in his words or his demeanour that could have caused the decision to go against him. It was the *Maestro's* whim, or the curse of his duties, or maybe, just maybe, the will of the silent young woman whose importance maybe, just maybe, he had underestimated and thus, unwittingly, slighted. He would never know. Collalto commiserated but, feeling the icy blast of Gianluca's humour all too clearly, remained as much out of sight, out of earshot, as their common duties allowed.

Nevertheless, some five or six days after Gianluca had taken his tumble, it became his friend's lot, yet again, to be the bearer of glad tidings.

It fell out thus. Arriving late at the Chancellery – an event which had almost assumed the cloak of habit – Gianluca was pounced upon by his friend, bursting with excitement. There was a message. From the *Maestro*. Could he please call to see him at his earliest convenience. So overjoyed was he at the likely prospect and meaning of these tidings that he did not think to inquire as to their provenance. But the morning dragged slowly by. The pile of letters brought for him to copy and to file away seemed never to reduce, even though he wrote frenziedly in the hope of making the time pass more swiftly. Master Niccolò appeared to be in a state of some consternation yet again – these days not uncommon, Gianluca had observed – and was thus more pernickety than usual about accuracy and neatness, returning no fewer than four letters to be recopied. "Festina lente!" he urged the young man, wagging his finger from side to side, like an inverted pendulum, "I have told you many times before; if speed and accuracy are at variance one with another, 'tis the former must give way! Save time, Master Gianluca, by giving more time!" And away he went, back to his office, with Gianluca's barely concealed anger shooting darts into his retreating back.

Yet, the endless morning did reach its end eventually, and the young man dashed away without so much as a word to his fellows. He half ran, half skipped, the length of Borgo de' Greci, so that by the time he was banging on the *Maestro's* door his pulse was racing, his lungs were aching, and despite his great impatience, he was indeed thankful that quite some minutes elapsed before the dour servant woman finally drew back the bolts and swung the door open to admit him once again.

Entering the room at the top of the house, he was immediately aware that its character had changed quite dramatically, in spite of the same blinding intensity of light coming from the window as had greeted him on his former visits. Some way to the right of the door, more or less in the centre of the room, was a huge, canopied bed with sumptuous crimson hangings cascading down from its peaked baldaquin, and this, because of its bulk, obscured most of the rest of the room. The *Maestro*, however, was silhouetted against the open window, as before, and slightly to his right a large studio easel blocked out some of the sun's early-afternoon blindness.

"I am so grateful, young man, so very grateful; especially after the evident disappointment I caused you in our last, brief encounter. I found, however, that I had made an unquestionable error in my choice of model – some people are impossible to work with in my profession, they yield so little – and, on reflection, I decided that, despite the inconveniences your employment in the Chancellery may be cause of, nevertheless, you might serve my purposes to much greater effect. Can I count on you still?"

Gianluca could in no way conceal his gratitude, nor his satisfaction… nay, his joy, and proclaimed himself ready to assist the *Maestro* to the very best of his ability.

"Then shall we begin at once?" the *Maestro* inquired. Although he had not expected it, Gianluca readily assented. "Then please, take a seat, and I shall explain briefly what my project is." Coming round the end of the bed, passing in front of the *Maestro*, he saw that there were two of the chairs from last time, set side by side, and that one of them was already occupied by a lady, almost certainly the one who had occasioned his confusion. As he approached to sit, she turned her head towards him and smiled, and seeing her, only now, for the first time, he was startled at her very great beauty, even though – he surmised – she was no longer in the first bloom of youth. He sat beside her and smiled back, again confused, unsure of what he should say to her, if anything at all. Mercifully, the *Maestro* came to his rescue. "This canvas, *Gli spossati per l'amore* (Worn out with Love), has been commissioned by a very great nobleman, to celebrate his ascendancy – an event which, he assures me, is to happen quite, quite soon." Gianluca was so charmed by the soft sibilants, the curtailed vowels, of the Venetian's speech, that he only half heard what he was saying. In any case, his painterly inner eye was already speculating on the possible nature of the picture to be painted, the *sposati per l'amore* (married for love) – it would have to suggest the harmony, peace and purity of the married state, the perfect *connubio*, itself a metaphor for the way the estate or whatever it was would be, once the said nobleman had come into his own... The disposition of the furniture, such as there was, led one to expect the married couple side by side, his hand laid upon hers on one of the chair arms, with the bed – and its pure white linen – in the background. At this juncture, he looked round, perhaps with the half intention of checking his conjecture against reality, and was quite startled to find that the 'pure white linen' was both crumpled and distinctly grubby, the counterpane was hanging over the bottom of the bed, while the blanket had been cast carelessly over to one side. What could it all mean? Perhaps, he concluded, he should concentrate more on the *Maestro's* explanation than on his own flights of fancy. And with this return determined, he was just in time to hear the artist declare, "That, then, is my purpose. Are you both content with it?"

Having heard nothing, he was at some disadvantage and shot a glance in the direction of the lady. Reassured by her nodding, he smiled, then said decisively (as if he had been elected to speak for the two of them), "We are content." The *Maestro* looked distinctly relieved at his words, which pleased him greatly. He was just about to add that he would be honoured to assist in the fulfilment of so interesting a project, when the *Maestro*, himself smiling a little by this time, confessed, "I was a little worried that as this was the first time you had ever posed, you might feel… well… embarrassed." Eager to please him, Gianluca spread his arms and then his hands wide in a gesture of reassurance. "Not at all!" he exclaimed and then, for good measure, more vehemently, "Not at all!"

"Then let us lose no more of the light," the painter urged, "let us begin at once". The lady rose and Gianluca did the same, affecting the same enthusiasm as the *Maestro*, though in truth – as we have seen – he had not the faintest notion of what would unfold. The lady was moving away to the far corner of the room and the young man was on the point of following her when he saw she was heading towards a large screen which, until now, because it was in the shadows, had completely escaped his notice. Such screens he had seen often enough in his sisters' rooms, and that of his parents; such screens, in his lore, betokened maidenly modesty and virtue. He checked his movement and stood looking helplessly at the artist who was busying himself behind the easel. After a moment or two, the

Maestro glanced in his direction and, in some obvious bewilderment, inquired, "Was there something you wanted to ask?" Gianluca shook his head and smiled yet again, a rather foolish smile, he felt, before affirming, "No, nothing, only…" and his words tailed off into silence. "Then hurry and remove your clothes, we have not a moment to lose if we are to complete the preliminary sketches today", and as he spoke the *Maestro* was pointing back over the young man's shoulder. Gianluca half turned to see an identical screen to that presumably designated for the lady, placed in the shadowy corner behind him. He looked back towards the *Maestro* who, unfortunately, had once again disappeared behind the easel. He felt beads of perspiration prickling his forehead; he knew nothing at all except that, for some obscure reason (oh, why, oh why had he not paid attention?) he was to take off his clothes and, it suddenly came to him, the lady was to do the same. He stood behind the screen, his pulse racing, uncertain what he should do. Only a few paces away was the door, and freedom, and his instinct urged him in that direction. He peered cautiously round the screen and saw that the *Maestro* was still busy behind the easel. He stepped quietly forward but then, just two or three steps from the door, he saw the lady appear suddenly, moving gracefully, easily, entirely naked, in the space between the end of the bed and the easel. He stood and stared at her, quite transfixed. He had never seen a woman naked before, unless once he had caught a glimpse of Lucrezia, his elder sister, as he passed, and paused, before her door, which was ever so slightly ajar, and yet of that scene he had never been entirely sure, so fleeting was its moment.

But here was beauty indeed, the pearl white vision of a heavenly dream. He hurriedly stepped back behind the screen and began throwing off his clothes, yet as he did so, he became aware that his own unruly flesh was astir and try as he may he could do nothing to quell it. The vision refused to fade, indeed, it intensified the more he sought to dismiss it, and by the time he was completely naked his pulsing member stuck out rigidly before him, like a dart, seemingly having a mind and a purpose quite independent of his own. He sat down on the stool provided, in some consternation. What ever was he to do? Cruelly, as if to compound his agony, came the urgent voice of the *Maestro*, "Ho there, young sir, I say, Gianluca, my fine fellow, here is a lady awaits you, trembling with cold; what delays you there sir?" And not knowing how to answer, the young man kept silent, and thus it was that the *Maestro*, part out of curiosity, part out of impatience, hastened over towards the screen. Gianluca, hearing his approaching steps, hastily dropped his cast-off hose over his predicament, but too hurriedly, for the legs parted round it, as if hanging from a rail, and immediately the artist pushed his way behind the screen he had the answer to his question. "Ah, young sir, there is place for neither stag nor unicorn in our picture; clearly you have mistook!" And he began to laugh loudly, calling back over his shoulder to the lady, "Now here's a fine sight that will surely set you a-trembling; indeed there is." Then, turning to face the crimson-faced young man once again, he said, still laughing quite uncontrollably, "And here's a further inconvenience, not in our contract! A pitcher of water should douse your flames", and with that he withdrew, presumably to prepare his remedy.

But just then, there came a shout from the street below, followed by another, then the sound of horses' hooves, more shouting of more voices, then the ring of steel on steel; of someone discharging a firearm; which action was immediately followed by a scream that was rapidly submerged in the ever-growing commotion. It sounded as if the whole of Florence were concentrating in the short, narrow street beneath the window. Gianluca leapt to his feet and peered over the top of the screen, to see the *Maestro* leaning out of the window, looking first in one direction then in the other. Unable to contain his curiosity, and quite forgetting his own affliction, he bounded over to the window to witness that of others below, as naked as in the hour of his birth.

In truth, it seemed as if two armies had met and joined battle. Great indeed was the confusion, but when his eyes had adjusted to the intensified light,

Gianluca saw that a goodly number of the combatants wore the livery of Master Niccolò's citizen militia, and it was they who appeared to have the upper hand. A rag-tag group of men armed with staves and the odd blade was clustered around a man on a black horse, seemingly trying to prevent the militia from reaching him. He himself was seeking to back his horse away in the other direction from the oncoming soldiers and, after a moment or two, he managed to break clear of the mass, turn his horse, and spur it into a gallop, soon rounding the corner at the end of the street. His erstwhile protectors then began to fall back in the same direction, the militia pressing hard upon them, but once the street end was near they too broke and fled in all directions, every man for himself, with the soldiers in hot pursuit.

When something like calm had returned, with only clusters of bystanders conversing, conjecturing, pointing and gesticulating down below, the *Maestro* drew his head inside once more, but, Gianluca noted, he was visibly shaken by those events. He went towards the bed where, Gianluca only now realised, the lady had been lying, swaddled in a sheet, all the while, and there he sat down heavily, his head in his hands. The lady moved towards him, abandoning her makeshift robe, and, pointing in the direction of the easel, commanded that Gianluca bring a cup of water from the pitcher there. Turning to obey, the young man suddenly remembered that this was undoubtedly that selfsame pitcher of water which, only minutes before, had been destined for another charitable mission, albeit of a different cast. He looked down and sighed his relief; like the rag-tag combatants of the street fracas, his own disturber of the peace had retreated quite out of sight.

The *Maestro's* humour had indeed been much affected by the affair in the street, so much so that he declared himself quite unable to proceed that day. Apologising profusely for the inconvenience this decision caused his sitters, he insisted on remunerating them at once. He rose unsteadily to his feet, still trembling visibly, and crossed the brief space to the easel and the little table that stood between it and the window wall. He returned without delay to drop three silver florins into Gianluca's hand, thanking him for his pains and suggesting he dress quickly, lest he take cold. This advice he followed, not forgetting to offer up a prayer of thanks to the Madonna, for his timely deliverance. Once ready, he came out from behind the screen, but seeing no one there he called out his valedictions, to which, still invisible, the *Maestro* replied, ascertaining also that the young man would be able to arrive at the same time on the morrow.

Returning homewards, Gianluca pondered the strange sequence of events of that curious afternoon. Quite apart from his embarrassment which, he knew full well, could have been very much greater had not Heaven intervened, and which, he was not unaware, was likely to plague him on future visits, there was the question of the *Maestro's* sudden discomfiture. What had been the cause of it? he wondered. The man did not give the appearance of one who would easily take fright at a street brawl, and especially one witnessed from a position of unassailable security. Curious indeed! Then there was the lady. Her demeanour suggesting not just ease but familiarity – very likely she had modelled for him before. Yet, had he not just arrived from Venice? And come to think of it, she certainly had not left by the time he himself was ready to do so. Who was she, then? His mistress, maybe? And another thing; why should a canvas entitled *Gli Sposati per l'Amore* (Married for Love) require that its protagonists appear completely naked? But here, he decided, he must defer to the greater wisdom of its creator who was, after all, a master of his craft. Besides, if it afforded him the continual pleasure of looking upon the lady's exquisite beauty un-censured, he for one would hardly complain. But there was something else that had perplexed him vaguely at the time, he remembered, but could not readily call it to mind now. And as he went along he wrestled with an unyielding memory, but to no avail. Indeed, it was to be some hours before the mists cleared in his head and the conundrum revealed itself in all its triviality and, as it turned out, uncertainty.

It happened while he was at meat with his family, though still pondering over the afternoon's events, only vaguely aware of the conversation that was going on around him. Suddenly, he realised, he was being recalled from his reverie: "Ho there, Gianluca, I say…" and it was these very words that echoed across his memory, as well as the table, to present him with the point that had so far eluded him. He was almost certain, but could not be so entirely, that when he had sat trembling behind the screen, the *Maestro*, in calling to him, had used his name; yet, so far as he remembered, he had never declared it to him, for the need to do so never seemed to arise. So how could the *Maestro* have known? Or perhaps he was mistaken after all, had indeed misheard; it was more than likely considering the state of great agitation he was in at the time.

On the following day, the events of the previous afternoon were sharply recalled, though the specific reference was in itself oblique, in a letter which Master Niccolò dictated, to be sent to the Florentine Ambassador in Rome, Signor Acciaiuoli.

The city, by all reliable accounts, is being infiltrated by spies and agents provocateurs in the pay of both the French and the Spaniards, and yet the Signoria fails continually to take decisive action. Afraid of offending everyone by any action it may embark upon, it ends by pleasing no one. The policy of 'wait and see', rather than aligning with one or other of the Leagues – which would at least afford some protection should matters take a turn for the worse – is sheer folly; but then, trying to steer a middle course between Scylla and Charybdis was ever thus. It is rumoured that there are many here who are dissatisfied, having lost patience with a government which seemed to promise much but which, though in office for nigh on fourteen years, has reputedly temporised in almost everything. I think it unlikely that we are about to witness revolt from within but I strongly suspect that if it were precipitated by external events, there would be no shortage of influential citizens who would flock to such a cause; certainly, the Medici have never lost their following, even if their apologists have remained largely silent until of late.

Although these matters were of small concern to Gianluca, he seemed to recall his father making not dissimilar observations on more than one occasion in recent weeks, shaking his head gravely and lamenting the deleterious effect the general air of unrest was having on his business affairs. Perhaps, after all, Gianluca conceded, this was more than just another instance of his father's seemingly endless devotion to carping and complaint. Thinking about it yet again, it was very likely that *Maestro* Lorenzo's apparently extreme reaction to yesterday's violence had its roots in not dissimilar concerns to those of his father. Certainly, such conjecture seemed far from fanciful; or so he reasoned. However, much to his disappointment, shortly before he was about to depart for his afternoon appointment, a young boy arrived bearing a message from the *Maestro*, explaining that he had suddenly been called away on urgent business and did not anticipate being at home again until after the weekend.

What to do with himself was a problem. He tidied his desk, slowly, unwontedly, and was almost the last to leave the office. He wandered off in the direction of the river and for a while stood looking at its meagre, thirsty course, reduced almost to a trickle in the centre, but finding nothing there to arrest his interest, away he drifted again. A sudden return to consciousness of his surroundings found him in Piazza Santa Croce where, out of the blue, or so it seemed, the idea entered his head that he might pass the *Maestro's* house on his way home; it was but a little out of his way and, in any case, he was in no hurry to be anywhere at all. Nevertheless, it vaguely troubled him that he felt the loss of he was not too sure what, so keenly, that he was drawn to the house even when he knew there would be no one there.

But he was wrong.

As he turned into the short, narrow street heading for Via delle Vecchie Stinche, he was just in time to see two - at least two - men entering the house whose door had closed by the time he drew level with it. He went on to the other end, surprised by what he had seen, then crossed the street at the corner before looking back. He saw at once that the mansard window was wide open and that two figures were leaning with their backs against the sill. One of them was almost certainly the artist. He watched for a moment or two but realising how compromising that would be, if he were spotted, he went on his way, perplexed and even more downcast than before, when the message had come for him at the office. It would be at least another four days before he could legitimately go there again – for a young man, impatient and eager, an abyss of time. But why had the *Maestro* uttered such an unnecessary untruth?

The days did, of course, pass by, but slowly, tediously, and his moroseness was commented on more than once at home. His sisters, teasing and taunting him, declared that such a mood could only come from some great passion and demanded to know who the lady was. Irritated, then angry, he swore at them and drove them giggling from his room, but they gave him no respite thereafter during the whole weekend. But, he had to admit to himself, they were possibly right in their assumptions, or at least, not very far wrong, but being scrupulously honest with himself, he had to recognise that it was – as yet – the lady's body he suffered for, since it was all he knew of her.

Come Monday, he was uncertain what to do; should he await the *Maestro's* summons or go to the house at the usual time, explaining his importunity by the lack of precision of the message he had received? After a morning of many errors and clearly straining the patience of Master Niccolò to the very limit, he decided he could not bear to live another day without seeing her. Thankfully, as it happened, he was expected, and the lady was already divested of her garments, wearing only a thin wrap tied loosely at the waist with a cord. The painter's sombre mood had, of course, passed, and indeed he appeared to be in the most jovial of spirits. "Quickly, then, out of your clothes, and to work, and pray that we have none - none, he repeated - of the problems we encountered on your last visit." Gianluca smiled wanly, retired behind the screen, and was naked in a trice. But speedy though he was, he was outpaced by the devil stirring between his legs, and once again he was thrown into a quandary: should he make a dash for the window and hope that the business of arranging the scene would take his mind off what his imagination fixed on like a leech, or should he prevaricate behind the screen until the swelling had subsided? Without really coming to any decision he found himself standing beside the bed, his hands seeking to conceal what his mind had failed to banish. The *Maestro* glanced in his direction from behind the easel, winked volubly at the lady who sat on a chair, still in her robe, with her legs curled up beneath her, then said, almost as if speaking to himself, "Do you not realise, Master Gianluca, that you will carry little conviction as one of the two *spossati per l'amore* (who are worn out by love) if you are unable to bridle the beast? Fortunately, perhaps, if all else fails, the paint brush will conveniently castrate thee! But we fervently hope it will not come to that." The lady could not contain her laughter, nor Gianluca his blushes, yet the devil remained unmoved by words, blushes or laughter. But whatever could the *Maestro* have meant with his comment about 'conviction' and 'castration'? Gianluca's mind was in a spin.

The young man edged away slightly, perhaps hoping that the bedpost would shield him from the lady's gaze if he could but judge the angle aright, but to no avail, since she herself rose from her chair in that same moment and came towards him. The *Maestro* was once again busying himself behind the easel, though he spoke to the woman as she passed him, in tones too hushed, however, for Gianluca to catch the remark. The lady stood before him now and smiled. "It is a perfectly natural reaction. I understand. There is no reason why you should feel ashamed." And with that, she reached forward and pulled his hands aside, retaining hold of the left one to lead him round the end of the bed. Once there, she took off her own robe and threw it over the back of the chair. This done, she stood beside the young man and, addressing the artist, declared, "We are ready."

Regaining a little of his composure, because of her kindness, Gianluca suddenly realised, in a flash, how he had been so cruelly misled, if not exactly betrayed, by Collalto's father's impatience with detail and, ruefully, his own failure to listen when the artist had outlined his project. But even so, even now, there seemed to be no distinction made in the Venetian's pronunciation of *spossati* (exhausted) and *sposati* (married), except... except that (he now suddenly realised) he had never heard him utter the latter of the two words, had merely presumed... What folly! And all for what? A deep and apparently recurring sense of embarrassment, the awakening of feelings which, if momentarily pleasurable, plunge him continually into a state of black anxiety, and not a word yet about his own aspirations in the world of art... What was he to do?

"Good!" declared the *Maestro*, appearing from behind the easel, wiping his hands on a piece of cloth, which he soon discarded on one of the chairs. "Let us arrange the scene." And with this he pulled the pillows and the bedclothes into a studied chaos, while the two stood watching, still hand in hand. "The woman figure will lie on the right, the man figure to her left. She on her back, a pillow under her head, he on his side, facing her. Can we try that, first of all? Then we'll make any finer adjustments once I have studied that initial disposition." The two of them clambered onto the bed and lay down as the *Maestro* had required. Once this was done, the latter moved around the bed, looking first from one position, then from another. Then, after a pause in which he regarded them still, though clearly deep in thought, he asked Gianluca to move his legs nearer to those of the lady and, indeed, to thrust his left leg between hers. Whether or not the lady was as coolly divorced from these intimacies as was the artist, the young man could not be sure, but for him it was clearly not so. The mere feel of her legs pressing on his own set his pulse racing and if there had been some slight subsidence of his manhood in the intervening moments, a sudden surge of desire made it jerk visibly. The lady turned her face into the pillow and he could feel her shaking with laughter. Quickly, however, she checked herself, and turned once more to face him, engaging his eyes, even at that most awkward angle. Then quite gently, imperceptibly almost, she covered the offending flesh with her hand. For Gianluca this agony was ecstatic, this ecstasy pure torment. He was sure it was more than his flesh could bear. He felt himself moving towards her, wanting to take her, to enter her immediately. He turned his head towards her but saw to his dismay that she lay there quite unmoved, her eyes open, looking in his direction, yes, but not seeing him. "Master Gianluca," then came the distant voice of the artist, "you have altered your position. You must not do so. I cannot paint your body if you move. Back, please, to your former position and, I implore you, stay there." And thus, at long last, the painting, *Gli spossati per l'amore,* was finally under way.

Once he had completed the initial layout and sketch, the *Maestro* chatted easily and generally with his two models, commenting on the news of the day, inviting their opinions, lingering a while over the growing sense of crisis in the peninsula, with the

French and the Spanish armies roaming and plundering at will, yet all agreed that Florence was undoubtedly the safest place to be; indeed, confided Master Lorenzo, it was for this very reason that he had gone to the expense, not to mention the dangers of the hazardous journey, of moving thither from Venice, for once embarked upon this commission he wanted neither interruptions nor anxieties before it was finished.

"And yet..." the younger man volunteered, if rather hesitantly, "and yet" he began again, clearing his throat as he did so. Master Lorenzo appeared surprised by this half intervention; "And yet?" he echoed. "Well," said Gianluca, "according to the correspondence with our ambassador in Rome, during the past week or so, things go less well with us than would appear." He had intended to say no more than this but seeing the all-too-visible alarm his remark had caused the *Maestro*, he felt he must qualify his statement by supplying some little detail of what he knew. "From the letters I have seen, it appears that the city is being infiltrated by spies from all sides; some are known suspects, and are watched, but there are others who are not, and these are much feared." The *Maestro* nodded his understanding, then after a brief pause suggested that such things were normal in times of unrest and that governments paid far more attention to them than, in reality, they warranted. Gianluca was a little put out that the intelligence he had volunteered was blown away so easily and after a moment or two's hesitation he went on: "That may indeed be so, I cannot say. However, apart from this matter, there is also that of our non-alignment which, to some, appears our greatest strength, but to others is a definite sign of weakness since, far from being a deliberate choice is the result of grave divisions and hesitancy in the councils. Each of the major powers has its champions and its detractors but none is strong enough to persuade and unite the others, or even a majority of the others. Thus, we lurch along from day to day, hoping against hope that something will happen well away from Florence that will, quite incidentally, secure our future. What is feared more than anything else is that a decision for decisive action will soon be required here because whatever it was, it could not come from a position of strength; it would be made without conviction."

"This sounds more serious," the artist acknowledged, to the young man's satisfaction, "but what is the feeling for the situation in the Chancellery?" he inquired.

"Well, in our section, there is great unease. Master Niccolò, who is responsible for keeping many channels of information open, is beside himself with anger at this paralysis which grips our government; he is forever railing against the folly of what he calls 'the middle way'. His opinion is never sought, however, for when all is said and done he is merely an executor of decisions made by higher authority." Then, to underline his point, and maybe, just a little, a sense of his own importance, he added, "From all of this, it appears that we should not be too complacent in our sense of security."

The *Maestro* was silent for a time, doubtless wrestling with some problem of his craft. "Master

Gianluca," he said, at length, "could you please turn your body slightly towards the lady and place your left hand on her breast, at the same time, looking deeply into her eyes?" The young man complied but immediately he felt a stirring and clearly, the lady felt it too, for she clasped him more tightly with the hand which had not left the wilful creature free to roam for one moment since the session had begun. The trouble was, occasionally, in order to alleviate a growing stiffness in her fingers, she would relax her hold, turn her hand, inadvertently stroking him, seeming to caress, and whatever beneficial effect they might have for her stiffness these few gentle movements merely recharged his own. But this latest request threatened to push him to the very limits of endurance. Feeling the hitherto merely imagined, merely craved-for, firm roundness of her breast beneath his hand for the first time, he did not know how to resist the temptation of probing and stroking with his fingers, seeking the nipple and caressing between fingers and thumb, actions which, he found, were powerfully addictive and which left him helplessly hoping against hope that the *Maestro* would not notice, or that the lady would not protest. Looking into her eyes (as had also been requested) he implored her indulgence and to his dismay and delight felt her hand relax and caress him gently, while her eyes which, not long before had seemed to look through him, were now alight, smiling in joy into his own. And if these signs had not been enough to convince him of her complicity, she pursed her lips tightly and mouthed him a tender kiss.

All of a sudden, the burning desire that the close proximity of her divine flesh constantly stoked up within him, was joined by another sort of desire, perhaps more a hope than a desire, that she too craved much more of him than had hitherto been made apparent by her words and actions. Yet, if she too were scorched by these fires of Hell, she gave no sign of it. The sitting – or lying – came to an end all too soon, though thankfully he was to return the very next day, and before he knew it, he was once more wrapped up in his divine agony.

Gently caressed, unable to prevent his mind – and his fingers – from wandering; wondering, wondering… He was jerked away from his tormented musings by the rasping voice of Master Lorenzo: "This Master Niccolò, you speak of. Is he not the one who was responsible for the formation of the famous citizen militia?" Gianluca gazed with great intensity into his lady's eyes, as if seeking her permission to divert his being from her bidding for the briefest of moments. Seeing the radiance of her smile as luminous as ever, never flickering for an instant, he mouthed a kiss at her before turning his head to answer the *Maestro* in a brief affirmative. Alas! This did not suffice, for the latter persisted with his train of thought aloud: "I thought it must be so. But this militia which, they say, he drills and trains personally, surely it will prove a formidable opponent should – God forbid! – we ever come to that pass?"

As if commiserating with him in this latest torment, his lady caressed him anew, so sweetly, so gently, that his ache (quite contrary to her intentions, he had no doubt) was doubled, becoming acutely physical as well as of his spirit. He had to stiffen his whole body into a death-like rigidity to avoid spilling his seed there and then upon her hand. He winced at the physical pain this superhuman effort of will had caused him. And yet she continued to smile like an angel, oblivious of the agony her kind gesture had inflicted upon him.

The pain abating somewhat, the young man forced his mind towards an answer. "The much-vaunted militia, of which there has been so much talk – talk which the government has actively encouraged, I might say – is unfortunately far from formidable, a fact which Master Niccolò himself is the first to concede."

The *Maestro* was genuinely surprised at this intelligence and inquired what, precisely, had occasioned these observations. Gianluca searched his memory, trying to recall the exact words his master had used on the very topic only the day before: "Well," he began again, "for one thing, it is starved of funds and is thus badly armed and but poorly prepared. The government was delighted with the idea of an efficient fighting force at a fraction of the cost of the usual mercenary army, but once it had got used to its delight, it then apparently set about fractioning the fraction - or so Master Niccolò complains."

"Oh, what folly!" Master Lorenzo exclaimed in heartfelt outrage, "such cheese-paring must have a disastrous effect upon morale…"

"Indeed, yes", Gianluca concurred. "If among some sections of the force there is great enthusiasm, the kind of patriotic fervour Master Niccolò himself envisaged as its likely main strength, there are many others who do not take it at all seriously. Many fail to present themselves at the training ground, or come spasmodically, or late; even the officers, who should be setting an example, cannot be relied upon."

"What then is to be done?" the artist asked, as he selected another brush and laid on yet more colour. Gianluca remembered a working paper that the Council of Eight had circulated on the subject some little time ago.

"Well, one solution that has been suggested is that for able-bodied men between the ages of sixteen and forty-five, training for the militia become obligatory and that failure to discharge those obligations satisfactorily incur a fine and, in cases of persistent neglect, even imprisonment."

And thus the conversation continued easily, back and forth, until a cooler air, coming from the windows, heralded the onset of the first shadows, bringing the session to a close.

If the *Maestro's* line of conversation served to curb his continually welling desires, the moment it ceased they returned with a vengeance. How could it not be so, with so divine a being cleaving to his flesh and, at the same time, penetrating the depths of his very soul with her bright shining eyes, which surely, oh surely, gazed as hungrily as did his own? Before they rose from the bed, this time she leaned towards him and placed a kiss lightly upon his brow, then instantly pulled swiftly away, at the same time releasing her hold upon his rebellious part, as one might after un-hooding a serpent or a falcon. All in one bound she was on her feet and moving rapidly towards the screen as the serpent reared its head, the falcon soared, and Gianluca groaned. And this – with only slight variations – was to be his fate for the following three sessions, alternately indulged and abruptly snatched from his swelling desires, while the *Maestro's* picture too grew apace, with new, often intimate details being added at each sitting.

At the end of his subsequent visit, as he was dressing, a plan was taking shape in his brain. He would leave at once, as if in a hurry to be elsewhere, but would then wait for his lady coming out, to follow her and, if the opportunity presented itself, to confront her, to importune her with his desires, with his undying love – and... came the afterthought... to ask her name.

As his hand reached for the catch on the door, he shouted his farewells, but Master Lorenzo, calling his name, "Oh, Master Gianluca, Master Gianluca, not so fast", came towards him, proffering – as he never failed to – the three silver florins which were his due. The young man thanked him, bowed deeply, ascertained that they would meet again in two days' time, and went on his way.

At the end of the street, however, he crossed Via delle Vecchie Stinche and entered a *fiascheria* where he ordered a cup of wine and settled down near the open door to watch the *Maestro's* house. Expecting that his wait would be a short one, he soon tossed off the wine, but as she did not then immediately appear he ordered another cup. But the shadows in the street began to lengthen, and still she did not come. The landlord tried to engage him in conversation when he brought his second cup, but Gianluca, anxious not to miss his lady, would not be drawn, keeping his ripostes as brief as courtesy would allow. The shadows thickened into darkness and the darkness into night, rush lamps and candles flickered into light, the street began to empty, and by the time Gianluca had downed his third cup he had decided she would not come, she was, after all then, the *Maestro's* mistress. He rose to his feet, paid the reckoning, and stepped unsteadily out into the darkness, disconsolate and bewildered, quite at a loss to explain her behaviour towards him.

For their next meeting, two days later, the young man resolved upon a cold hauteur towards her, since his conviction about her status, not unnaturally, caused her to tumble headlong from the lofty pedestal she had – all unbeknownst to herself – come to occupy in his thoughts during this past week or so. His first remarks he addressed exclusively towards the *Maestro*, as though she had ceased to exist – and, in fact, it must be reported that she was, as yet, nowhere to be seen, though Gianluca had no doubt at all that she would be close at hand. However, even by the time he was naked and ready to commence the session she had not yet appeared. As the *Maestro* had also, apparently, left the room, he sat down on the corner of the bed and waited. The longer he sat there, however, the more uneasy he felt, though he was unable to explain to himself why it should be so. After several minutes had elapsed and still no one had entered, he rose and, led by curiosity, ventured behind the easels which were acting as supports for the huge canvas. Although there was not sufficient space between it and the window wall for him to step far enough away from it to see the whole picture properly, he was nevertheless struck immediately by the fineness and mastery of the detail, the powerful contrast between the brightness in the foreground and the increasing penumbra the deeper into the picture his eye moved. But what impressed him most of all was the steep, certainly novel perspective the artist had achieved by foreshortening his figures where they lay. His own features were not visible, since his position, facing the lady but with his back to the painter, determined that they should not be so, yet the lady was unmistakably who she was, as clearly as if the work had been intended as a portrait and not an allegory. He stood now gazing directly into her eyes, just as his reclining self had done on their last encounter, and he felt his predetermined attitude melting away in their depths, before she had even experienced its coldness and been forced to reflect upon its possible cause or meaning. He found himself trembling and he was not sure whether out of a suddenly rekindled desire for her or for fear that she would not come, that something had prevented it, had happened to her, and he panicked, rushing out from behind the canvas, intent upon calling the *Maestro* whose name was already forming upon his lips, and straight into the arms of his naked lady.

"What is it, Gianluca, what ails thee Gianluca, my love? Whither goest thou in such reckless, headlong flight?" And, as ever, it seemed, when he encountered this angelic being, he was thrown into confusion and incoherence.

"I was... I didn't... it was just that..." but he did not know how to go on, and he shrugged helplessly, shaking his head from side to side. She smiled up at him and, standing on tip-toes kissed him gently between the eyes and in doing so her cold, hard nipples seemed to burn their imprint upon his chest and he almost swooned in ecstasy. Alas! The moment was all too brief since, on hearing the door latch being lifted, the lady sprang back, out of his arms, declaring as she did so, "Ah, but here is the *Maestro*, if I am not mistaken", and indeed, she was not.

Master Lorenzo was in a merry mood, his eyes twinkling, his step sprightly. "A thousand apologies," he almost shouted, "for having kept you waiting, my friends", but he offered no explanation as to why it had happened. "Well, if you will resume your positions (he seemed to pause for a moment)… your positions upon the bed, we shall try and make some further progress." And without delay he set about his task. "As you have probably seen," he began again, "there is still some work to be done around the woman-figure's face and neck, and it is there we shall concentrate our attention this afternoon." Though he said not a word, Gianluca was quite content to do the same, and he smiled into her eyes, and her face lit up, briefly, in response, before settling back into the intense gaze the artist required and which, as the young man had seen just a moment or two before, he had already captured so precisely. "Incidentally" – the *Maestro* again, his head jerking out from behind the canvas, and with just a hint of rebuke in his voice – "we were beginning to think you were not to favour us with your presence today, were we not, Master Gianluca?" and with this his head disappeared once more as he, presumably, became absorbed once more in his labours.

"I would have sent word had it been so", she retorted, clearly put out by the reference to the, in truth, only very slight lapse of her habitual punctuality. "My mother, who has been unwell of late, needed my assistance just as I was leaving. I had to be sure she was comfortable, then call a neighbour to sit with her a while."

The painter offered no comment, indeed there was no indication at all that he had even heard, or listened to, her explanation, and the moment passed. Gianluca, however, was forced back to his thoughts and surmise of the previous occasion and had to acknowledge, in the light of the intelligence she had volunteered, that he had leapt in his frustration to quite the wrong conclusion. The artist would surely have known some of this if their relationship had been more intimate. At very least, it was clear that she did not dwell with him in that house, and his hopes revived once more of being able to see her, to talk with her, in some other place.

It was her hand, gently, playfully fondling him which brought him back to the reality, the absurd reality, of his situation. Glancing towards the window to make sure the painter's eyes were not upon them, she whispered, "Fickle young sir, have I lost your love so soon?" And he, wishing to reassure her a thousand, nay, a million times, of his ever-unchanging, ever-undying love, whispered the word "Never", then repeated it again, then again, and at the same time, in his turn, and quite imperceptibly, toyed gently with her nipple which, precisely as the picture demanded, lay conveniently to hand. This dalliance, however, did not go long uninterrupted, for the *Maestro* was in a jocund, talkative frame of mind, and Gianluca groaned inwardly at having to tear his attention away from his Aphrodite.

"Things go ill with the French, it seems, according to the latest news from the north," Master Lorenzo observed, and as he received no reply he soon went on, "rumour has it that they have been forced to quit Ravenna and Bologna and that now they are hard pressed even at Parma." And with this, he emerged from behind the painting to ask Gianluca whether or not he could confirm any of this. The young man sighed, then did indeed verify that this was the case, adding the conventional wisdom of the hour in the Chancellery, namely that "It is greatly feared that the Spanish infantry are unstoppable."

The painter shook his head, apparently in sorrow, "One wonders," he said, "where it will all end." And then, "With this sudden downturn in the fortunes of the French, the Florentine government must needs reassess its position, for what may have looked like relative security a week or two ago, now takes on the appearance of its very opposite. They will be forced to declare themselves one way or the other, for all of this now comes too close for comfort."

Gianluca agreed and then confided that even as they spoke the Ten of War were meeting in the great chamber in the Signoria to try and agree a contingency plan. With this intelligence vouchsafed, he expected the *Maestro* to press forward out of sheer curiosity, and thus he was much taken aback when instead he asked, "Well, Master Gianluca, how do you keep yourself amused... when you are not attending to affairs of state, that is... or lying with the maidens of Florence?" Although his face was hidden from the artist's gaze, that was not the case so far as his goddess was concerned, and he blushed deeply, not knowing whether he should offer a rebuttal of the *Maestro's* surmise or answer his question directly. After a moment's pause, he settled on the latter course.

"Well, sir, it may surprise you to know that I aspire to be an artist... like you, and thus, whenever the opportunity presents itself, I practise in my chamber," and then he added, "there, quite unsuited as it is, for the light is so poor, so as not to excite the wrath of my father, who has no time for art nor, indeed, for any of the divinely inspired works of any of the sacred Muses..."

He had expected at very least some encouraging remark from the artist and was quite nonplussed when his explanation was followed by a complete silence. After a minute or so, the *Maestro* came and stood at the foot of the bed, scrutinising them intently but not seeing *them,* only the problem they represented in that moment and in which he was so deeply absorbed. He returned then to his work, occasionally looking out from behind the canvas, and it was quite some time before he spoke again and when he did it was to say, almost absently, "Of these matters, we shall speak again presently", so that Gianluca was left wondering whether he had alluded to the artistic problems or to his own confession, or indeed, to the developing political discomfiture of the Florentine State.

When the session was over, the lady hurried away, as indeed Gianluca had presumed she would. In anticipation of this, he himself had dressed quickly in the hope of accompanying her and talking with her as they went, away from the impossible restrictions that their meetings here imposed upon them. But this was not to be, for as he was on the point of leaving, the *Maestro* engaged him in conversation precisely about his artistic aspirations, asking him what subjects he preferred to paint and whether or not he had ever received any instruction in the art. Indeed, just the kind of conversation Gianluca had formerly dreamed of having, the original purpose behind his being there at all. But not now. Not now. For his lady was his only concern in that moment, and she, he knew, was fast slipping away into the crowds, along unknown streets, to be lost to him yet again, until their next unsatisfactory contact in this place in three days' time. And when at last the *Maestro* brought their conversation to an end, he knew it was already too late, and he returned home disconsolate, and that despite the *Maestro's* offer to look at some of his paintings and the strong hint that he might, in due course, be looking for an apprentice for his workshop.

On the day of their next appointment, as he was coming along Via delle Vecchie Stinche, Gianluca was amazed to see his smiling lady coming towards him. Immediately, she took his arm and pulled him to one side, where they stopped and looked deeply into each other's eyes. "What detained you the other day? I waited at the end of the street in the hope that you might accompany me homewards, but you didn't come, and you didn't come and so I, anxious about my poor mother's well-being, was forced to hasten away."

The young man relived his anguish of then, even as she reminded him of her own, explaining how it had come about. She listened, smiling all the while, then declared, "Well, today, nothing will keep us apart. Whichever of us leaves first will wait at the corner of this street until the other shall come; then we shall while away the rest of the afternoon till dusk. My dear mother is quite restored and my preoccupations on her account are somewhat abated."

And so it was that their first tryst was sealed.

After his peremptory inquiry about the progress of Gianluca's painting since their last meeting, the *Maestro* changed the topic of their conversation abruptly to the events of the past few days. The young man was, of course, well aware of the momentous nature of the events unfolding even then around the Florentine city of Prato, not a dozen miles to the north, and of the panic, confusion and dismay the Spanish attack had occasioned among the ever-more inept-seeming rulers of the Republic. "Rumour has it," the painter remarked, "that though they have been so far victorious, the Spaniards are exhausted and very short of supplies, especially victuals, and that they would be well enough pleased to arrange a truce if the Florentine government were so disposed."

"It is indeed so," Gianluca confirmed, "but even now, at this eleventh hour, the Ten of War cannot come to a clear decision on what course of action they should follow."

"But is it not obvious? Florence now stands alone against the most powerful infantry in the world. They would do well to look upon the Spaniards' temporary discomfiture as a gift sent from Heaven!"

"Master Niccolò is of precisely that same opinion," the young man declared, "but there is growing support for defending the sacred honour of Florence - at whatever cost", and he shook his head sadly.

"Honour can prove a very costly business, and is like to do so in this affair. What then is being proposed?"

"Nothing to inspire much confidence, I'm afraid. There is only the Militia... ", and he shrugged, hopelessly. There followed further speculation by the *Maestro*, on the abilities of the Militia as a fighting force, and very detailed confirmation of his worst fears, supplied by Gianluca who, from the correspondence of the past few days had learned just how parlous a state the Militia, and therefore the fortunes of the city, was in. Then gradually, the conversation swung back to the painting and, when the session was over, the *Maestro* invited the two models to view his handiwork for the first time. Both of them marvelled and the young man was immediately aware of just how much the whole painting had changed in tone since last he had looked upon it. From the central figures there emanated a powerful glow, a brightness which almost caused one to turn one's head from it.

"One final sitting, the day after tomorrow – God, the Florentine government and the Spaniards willing – and it should be finished" the painter announced, clearly delighted with his work. This news was received with much less enthusiasm than it was given, the two models exchanging swift, panic-stricken glances. Suddenly, their situation had entered into a state of crisis to which they must find a solution at once.

By the time Gianluca had dressed, and he dressed quickly, his lady had already departed. Mindful of the delay visited upon him by the *Maestro's* conversation on the previous occasion, he determined to slip away, rude though it might be judged, without even a brief salutation; and this he did. As soon as he stepped out into the street, he saw her, true to her word, standing at the end of the street. She smiled and beckoned, and his heart soared. By the time he had come to where she had been standing, she herself was just about to turn into Borgo de' Greci, heading in the direction of the great Piazza; and she paused to look back, making sure that he saw which way she was going. When she saw him, she smiled once more; he waved, and away she went. He quickened his pace, to ensure that he had closed the gap between them by the time she reached the Piazza which, at that hour – that of the evening stroll, the *passeggiata* – would be churning with townsfolk. Sure enough, by the time he entered Borgo de' Greci, she had covered only half of the distance to the Piazza, and he saw her at once, over on the other side, walking quickly, but staying on the opposite side he had no difficulty keeping her in view. And once again, at the Piazza, she turned and looked back, searching, and when she saw him her face lit up once more and she raised her arm and he, his heart brimming with love and desire, waved back. Instead of plunging into the Piazza, however – as he, for no very good reason, he owned, had anticipated she would – she turned right in the direction of the river. When he, in his turn, stood where she had been a few moments before, at the entrance to the Piazza, his eyes moved (as experience by now had taught him they must) towards the end of the street which eventually overlooked the Arno, expecting to find her some way along, awaiting him.

But she was not there.

Rapidly, his eyes moved back along the street to where he stood, without seeing her. Two large, covered carts drawn by oxen, rumbled by him, headed towards the Piazza, for several moments obliterating his view of the other side of the street. He hurled himself past them, in the direction of the river, in order to reduce the time in which he was unable to see what was happening on the other side of the street, but to no avail. She was nowhere to be seen. In that moment, he lost his head, and began to run towards the river, bumping and jostling more sedate pedestrians as he went. Reaching the embankment, he looked up- and down-stream, hoping to catch sight of her, but again she was nowhere to be seen. He crossed the *Lungarno* to the river itself, and looked down, but there was no way she could have got down there so quickly, and he knew he had lost her. He hurried back the way he had come, in the direction of the Piazza, still hoping against hope to catch sight of her once again, but she had disappeared completely. Perhaps she had entered one of the houses along the street believing, mistakenly, that he had seen her do so, and he ran along first on one side, then on the other, to see whether any had been left ajar. Two of them had, one on each side of the street. He peered inside one of them, into a deserted courtyard. There was no way of knowing. He crossed the street and tried the other. Immediately behind it was a broad flight of stairs, which he climbed to the level of the first two or three doors which gave off it, but even if he had met anyone, what would he have said? He still did not know her name. He ran down to the street and went outside and there he leaned up against a wall, trying to fathom out what had gone wrong. He looked back across the road to the corner where he had last seen her. Then he understood. Though she had indeed gone right, much to his surprise, it had probably been only to find a gap in the throng of carts, horses and strollers, to then duck back and continue on into the Piazza and not in the direction of the river. Alas! Many minutes had now gone by and even if she had realised what had happened, it was unlikely that she would still be waiting for him, somewhere in the Piazza. None the less, he decided it was worth a try. Anything was. Anything was better than this milling desperation.

But she was nowhere to be found.

That evening, all the talk at the family table was of the impending political disaster. The government had not only repeatedly failed to take sensible precautions, following too close a French policy which, in the light of French defeats, had left the city isolated, but had continually failed to raise the necessary loans either to buy protection or to buy off the Spaniards. But, as Gianluca's father observed and certainly his own probably much greater sure knowledge of the political situation both within and outside the city confirmed, there were many in the city who were less than committed to the continuing existence of the Republic.

The old man had long been deeply critical of the Soderini, if not entirely of the republican ideal itself, but now revealed himself more gloomily resigned than critical; the return of the exiled Medici, in the wake of a Spanish victory, seemed inevitable. The news from Prato could not have been worse, its fall seemed imminent. There was even a rumour that some time that very day the Council of Eighty had strongly advised that the exiled Medici be allowed to return to the city, albeit as private citizens, in a last-ditch attempt to defuse the immediate crisis. Gianluca's father had heard too that Soderini had tendered his resignation but that this had been refused by the Signoria.

It was not until he had finally retired to his chamber for the night that Gianluca had the opportunity of thinking back over the whole afternoon's events and their eventual failure. Fortune, he decided, was decidedly, spitefully, set against him. Master Niccolò, he remembered, was always prating on about taking decisive action to limit the reach of Fortune, to hedge her in, thrust her back; indeed, there was no such active, malevolent force at all, merely chance, for good or ill. Be that as it may, what could he have done differently? What could anyone have done in the prevailing circumstances? The lady had simply been swallowed up in the rushing torrent of townsfolk which had swamped his dreams and hers, yet again. On the next occasion, there must be no room for error; they must leave together so that chance (or Fortune) should not slide between them.

The following morning, the city was in an uproar. When he arrived at the Signoria, he found it cordoned off, with groups of mainly young, heavily armed men, and a handful of Militia guards, preventing anyone from entering the building. He approached one of the groups and began to explain why he needed to gain entry, but they told him that today there would be no work done and that he had best return home until the morrow. A crowd had already gathered in the Piazza and new people were arriving every minute. He caught sight of Collalto and one or two more of the young men from the department and pushed his way through to them. "What's happening? Why is no one being allowed through?" he asked.

"Haven't you heard?" they replied in some amazement, "Prato has fallen and the Spaniards are on their way here. The Medici party have seemingly taken matters into their own hands. Rucellai, Neri Capponi, some of the Tornabuoni, Vespucci, and others we didn't see, have taken over the Signoria and, it is said, are even now closeted with Soderini and other high-ranking members of the government. There are going to be changes, that's certain, and probably drastic ones at that."

There were sporadic cries from different points in the crowd, mainly of "Long live the Republic!" and counter-cries of "Out with Soderini!" or "Long live the Medici!" Over to their left, a scuffle broke out between rival partisans, but this was quickly stamped out by one of the groups of armed men who, from their vantage point at the top of the steps, were able to spot trouble developing and deal with it before it got out of hand. Their action, however, did little to calm the mood of the crowd which, Gianluca sensed, was becoming more and more tense the longer they remained in ignorance of what was taking place and how it was likely to affect their own individual families and fortunes. Another fight broke out further back, this time more serious, it seemed, for you could hear the clash of steel against steel, and the crowd surged, presumably to make space for the combatants or, more likely, to get well out of their way.

Gianluca decided that this was no place to be and, bidding his colleagues farewell, he set off to return home. Once there, however, he could settle to nothing and spent most of the day wandering about the house, trying to calm himself, to think clearly about his future, making and remaking plans for himself and his lady for the morrow. By the end of the day it had become common knowledge that Piero Soderini and several of his close associates had left Florence for exile.

On the following day, there was already a large crowd gathered in the Piazza by the time Gianluca arrived there. The groups of armed men had been replaced by regular soldiers in strange uniform and huge, domed helmets and these, he surmised, must be the famed and much-feared Spanish infantry. People were being allowed in, he noted, and (more reassuringly) out of the Palazzo and, when he had finally made up his mind to try and enter he was merely waved through without having to give any account of himself. Although there were infantrymen everywhere, and especially standing in twos and threes outside almost all interior doors, none made any effort to obstruct him, not even those standing beside the entrance to the Chancellery. The normally silent room echoed with the babble of voices and here too the clerks and runners and one or two fellow-secretaries were huddled in groups, speculating on events. Master Niccolò had been there briefly but had at once been called away and, as it transpired, was not to reappear all morning. As a consequence, no tasks were allotted and little or no work was done. Time dragged its feet. The shadows cast by the light flooding in through the great balcony window appeared not to move.

Gianluca was beside himself with anxiety and impatience. He drifted from group to group but no one knew anything for certain. There were some who spoke openly of their satisfaction at the passing of the Soderini, hazarding the hope that the new government, once formed, would be more disciplined and organised and that law and order would once again take the place of anarchy on the streets of the city. Collalto, Gianluca noted, was one of these more outspoken critics of the former government, doubtless echoing his father's opinions, for had not their family always been boot-lickers of the *ottimati*, the most powerful families – or so his own father had always scornfully maintained. 'There are likely to be quite important changes even in this office, mark my words...' Collalto was predicting as Gianluca wandered away.

Although he had convinced himself that these momentous events in the life of the city were unlikely to have much, if any, effect on the tenor of his own life, they had none the less shaken him in some obscure way, so that he found himself longing not just for the touch and gaze and anticipation of his lady, but for the normality of the *Maestro's* studio and the ease and familiarity of its atmosphere.

Thus, released from the torpor of the morning, he swung jauntily away down Borgo de' Greci, determined that today he would not only elbow chance aside, and give it no rein at all so far as his love was concerned, but would approach the *Maestro* directly about his future as an artist, even maybe as apprentice to the *Maestro* himself. He was done with easy-going meekness, once and for all. As if to add conviction to his new resolution (whether for himself or those inside, was not very clear) he banged harder and longer on the outer door than had hitherto been his practice. After a while, the door was flung back by a tall young man whom he had never seen before and this, it has to be admitted, took him greatly by surprise. His resolution wilted into a stammered explanation of who he was and why he was there, and the fact that the young man showed not the slightest glimmer of understanding, deflated him even more.

"*Maestro* Lorenzo?" the young man repeated, "Never heard of him. Doesn't live here." He made as if to close the door and at this, Gianluca's habitual evenness of temper shattered. He leapt forward, put his shoulder to the door, forced his way inside and, without either backward glance or apology, ran up the familiar stairs three at a time.

By the time he arrived at the top landing he was gasping for breath, partly because of the exertion, partly out of anger and frustration. The door was slightly ajar and he jerked it open in his indignation, ready to denounce the stupidity of servants to the world at large; but he stopped, even before his speech had begun. The scene that greeted him was unbelievable. But if he was shocked by what he saw, it was all too obvious that his own intrusion was just as shocking. In the centre of the room was a large board, with several people seated around it, dining, with one or two of them arrested in mid-action, as they had lifted forkfuls of food to their opening mouths or raised a flagon to replenish a failing goblet. A woman looked up from a canopied cradle over which she was bending. A child of three or four years crawled out from beneath the table, climbed to its feet and waddled towards him, proffering a crust of bread which it held in its grubby fingers. His eyes swept the room. There was not a trace of anything he recognised. He backed out mumbling an apology and, as he turned to retrace his steps, he was passed by the youth, who leered into his face, entered the room and slammed the door behind him.

Gianluca stood staring at the door, wondering even now whether he had made a mistake, had not climbed far enough up the stairs, but it was the door right enough. There was no mistake. He felt suddenly faint with apprehension and had to cling hold of the banister to prevent himself falling. He sat down on the steps for safety, until the worst giddiness had passed. He could not begin to explain what had happened. How the central place and events of his life in recent weeks could suddenly have ceased to exist, as if they had never been, without trace. He rose to his feet, still feeling dizzy, and somehow, still clinging to the stair rail for support, he lurched down the steps and out into the bewildering street. He was at a loss to know what to do.

He retraced his steps of a couple of days before down towards Piazza Santa Croce, to the point at which he had lost sight of her. He crossed into the Piazza and stood on the corner for a time, looking first this way, then that. He walked along the road that led to the river and again stood there, looking in all directions. But he knew in his heart of hearts he was clutching at straws. And yet, he reasoned, even if the artist had quit the city, she must still be here somewhere; after all, she had the responsibility of her ailing mother. Surely she must be here, somewhere very close by, and with persistence and patience... And yet, she must either have known that the artist planned his sudden departure or she, like him, would have made the discovery, much as he had made it, when she called at the house for the final session...

Then it came to him from nowhere. Almost certainly, she had not been there by the time he had made his intrusion into the household now occupying the *Maestro's* studio, for if she had the youth, at least, however stupid and uncouth, would surely have remarked upon the coincidence… On the other hand, he had not given him much time to explain anything… Maybe the amazed silence of the family around the table had been occasioned by the fact of what might have been not the first but the second intrusion upon their repast. Fool that he was he had hurried away too soon, accepted the apparent too soon. He should have questioned them. He should have waited there in case she came. Perhaps even now she was walking along Borgo de' Greci in the direction of the Piazza. He would go and intercept her, meet her, throw his arms about her; surely, that was how it must be. And quickly, he crossed the street and headed back up towards Via delle Vecchie Stinche, expecting at any moment to see her crossing the road, turning the corner, her eyes everywhere, searching, like his own. But all too soon, he found himself standing once more looking into the heavy, blank face of the artist's door, having encountered no one. He resolved to gain entry once more, to question them, to find out whether they knew anything at all of the whereabouts of the artist or of the lady.

Once again, he began hammering upon the door. He stopped for a moment or two, to listen for approaching footsteps, but when no-one came he started his banging again, even more insistently than before. But no one came, and when he resumed his beating at the door a third time, people appeared from adjacent houses, windows were thrown open, and he was told, in no uncertain terms, that he had better desist forthwith or suffer the consequences. He tried to explain in his desperation, but no one would listen, and he was forced to quit the house and the street, as much in ignorance as he had been the first time.

That night, as his mind chased back and forth trying to make some sense of the mystery which had befallen him, he suddenly remembered that it had been his friend, Collalto, who had first introduced him to the painter, since the studio the latter had leased belonged to his father. It was very likely that he would have some news of him and of his departure.

Thus, on the following morning, he hastened to the Signoria to find out whatever Collalto knew. As he entered the building he became immediately aware that there was an unaccustomed throng of people in the foyer, crowding around something or other, but so much in a hurry was he that he gave no thought to the matter, nor was his curiosity in the least aroused to know the object of their attentions. On entering the great hall of the Chancellery, he realised that Collalto was not at his desk. He looked about but, failing to see him, he made for his own little room, deciding that he had not yet arrived. Before entering he looked back once more, to make sure he hadn't missed him, then, on turning to step into the room he came face to face with him, sitting there at his own desk, quill in hand. He stood and gaped for a moment or two, unable to comprehend. Was this some elaborate kind of joke perhaps? He presumed it must be and his face slipped into a smile. "Good morning, Mr Secretary," he jibed, "I trust I find you well? Indeed, you are the very… " but he was not allowed to finish. The inner door opened and Master Niccolò appeared with a sheaf of papers in his hand. "Ah, Master Gianluca, there you are", he said, somewhat lamely. For a moment or two he busied himself with explanations to Collalto, pointing first to one document, then to another; "so, if you would give this priority I should be most grateful," he concluded, then turning towards Gianluca he commanded, "If you would be so good as to step this way, Master Gianluca, I have some intelligence to impart to you." And with this, he went back into his own room. Gianluca's face clearly expressed his bewilderment but Collalto merely shrugged his shoulders and bent his head to his task. Gianluca followed Master Niccolò into his room and closed the door behind him.

"Please, Master Gianluca, be seated" the Secretary began. "As you have observed already, Master Collalto is sitting in your room and indeed is now occupying the post of secretary which, until now, has been your own." Here, he paused, awaiting the young man's reaction. Gianluca, for his part, was fully expecting him to continue, explaining (he supposed) the new post he had now been promoted to, and so did not interrupt.

"Master Gianluca, do you not say anything to your dismissal from your post? If you yourself have so little interest in the causes, I am certain that your father will require some explanation of you."

Gianluca could not believe his ears; "dismissal?" he repeated, "did you say 'dismissal'?"

Master Niccolò nodded gravely.

"It has been intimated to me by two or three persons of note, one of whom is a member of the Signoria, no less, that you have been guilty of certain… indiscretions and that you are not a fit person to be entrusted with the highly confidential business which passes through this office. I have therefore been instructed to terminate your employment, unless, of course, you tender your immediate resignation; in which case, the reasons need never be made public…"

The young man was on the point of protesting his innocence when the Secretary rose to his feet and moved quickly, on tiptoe, towards the door, which he suddenly threw open. He stepped through into the outer office and, finding Collalto still at his desk, asked him whether he had yet completed any of the more urgent letters. He then came back inside and shut the door once more, and resumed his seat. Leaning across the desk he spoke in markedly more hushed tones than before.

"One can never be too careful. The very walls are like to sprout ears from now on, I fear. But Gianluca, I am sorry that I have to be the enforcer of this ruling. There have been several changes made already since the fall of the government and, I am told, there are likely to be many more. I myself may not survive them. I do not know whether the charge of 'indiscretions' is fair or not – probably it is not – but the changes that are being made are of a political nature. Those who were, or who come from families known to be, partisans of the returning Medici, are likely to receive preferment in office. Pretexts for dismissal will always be found for anyone who stands in the way of such preferment. Explain this to your good father; he will certainly understand."

Gianluca nodded and rose to leave. "Should my resignation be in writing?" he inquired.

Master Niccolò also rose and, in the louder tones of before he answered, "Yes, it would be better if it were so."

The young man looked at him questioningly but the other had once more taken on the mantle of Florentine Secretary. "Good day to you, therefore, Master Gianluca. I trust you will let me have your note at your earliest convenience." Gianluca bowed peremptorily, turned on his heel, and left the room. He did not speak to, nor even look at, his erstwhile friend, nor did the latter deign to break his silence.

Slowly, because deep in thought, he came down the great staircase of the Signoria. When he reached the entrance hall, the crowd had thinned out somewhat and he was now able to see quite plainly what it was that had been the object of their curiosity. Supported on a large, heavy trestle, was the painting he knew so well, much better than any of the other onlookers could ever hope to know it, for it encompassed all his being, his aspirations, his suddenly imposed sense of never-ending loss. And yet, seeing it there, of all places, placed purposefully before the public eye, he was stunned. He glanced from side to side at the faces of others who were there admiring it, trying to see whether anyone recognised him as one of the two figures in the painting. And yet, he reasoned, it could not possibly be so, for in the picture his face was almost hidden; which was not the case with the lady, and he stared at her image, into the eyes his shadow self also gazed into and would do so for as long as ever the painting survived.

Eventually, he moved forward and stood close by it, reading the inscription that had been set upon it in black lettering upon a golden scroll: "Il Trionfo della Fortuna" (The Triumph of Fortune). He smiled at the change of title; at the picture's seeming change of fortune. Then he read also that the painting had been presented to "His Most High Excellency, the Magnificent Lorenzo de' Medici, by his many well-wishers in the Signoria and the High Councils of the Florentine State, in commemoration of his timely return to his native city, to rescue it from the decadence into which it has lately fallen". He smiled at that too, ironically, recognising that he also, all-unbeknowing, had been instrumental in that hypocrisy; nay, not hypocrisy, betrayal rather. He smiled bitterly when, in all humility, he was compelled to recognise also how he too had been betrayed. He turned and left the building, infinitely sadder, a little wiser, about the ways of his fellow men.

His returning home so early was cause of great consternation. His mother insisted that it must be because of some distemper and could not be made to understand that he had been dismissed. She then insisted, as did his sisters, that there must be a mistake – a case, maybe, of mistaken identity, as one of them suggested – and that once his father had spoken with Master Niccolò everything would be put to rights. Realising it was pointless trying to explain the circumstances he appeared to agree with them and declared that he would go to his room to read for a while. It was then that Bianca, his younger sister, remembered that a packet had been brought for him and she went to fetch it. When she returned, she made some play at keeping it from him, but he was in no mood for such frivolity and roughly he seized it from her. Instantly, she realised how she, indeed, how all three of them had underestimated the significance of what had happened to him, whatever it was. With tears flooding into her eyes, she apologised for her silliness and turned to leave. Seeing her distress, however, Gianluca melted, caught her by the arm and drew her to him, kissing her forehead. "I too am sorry," he said, then in a moment or two added, "when I am calmer, I shall tell you about the strange experience I have had. But not now. I cannot now." And he dried her tears with his kerchief. And so he entered his chamber.

The packet was small but heavy for its size. He opened it at his writing desk. Three silver florins fell out and rolled in different directions all over the leather-topped surface. He looked inside for a letter of explanation but there was none, only a couple of lines scribbled on a small, roughly-torn piece of paper:

'The tenth and final payment owed for the inconvenience caused you.

Your help has proved invaluable.

Now the wheel has thankfully come full circle.'

It was signed, 'Fortuna'.